# AFTER THE FALL

### Broken Angel
### Book 2

### L.G. Castillo

This book is a work of fiction. Names, characters, places, and incidents
are a product of the author's imagination. Locales and public names are
sometimes used for atmospheric purposes. Any resemblance to actual
people, living or dead, or to businesses, companies, events, institutions,
or locales is completely coincidental.

The binding scene is based on the classic hand binding ceremony:
Blessing of the Hands by Author Unknown.

Book Layout ©2013 BookDesignTemplates.com
Book Formatting: Polgarus Studio
Cover Design: Mae I Design

After the Fall/ L.G. Castillo
Second Edition: February 2014

De la espina y el dolor nace la flor.

(From the thorn and the pain a flower is born.)

~Spanish Proverb

# 1

Rachel's cloak fluttered as she sped through the dark tunnel. He was there. She could feel him.

Shivering, her fingers fumbled with the heavy material as she drew it closer to her body. Puffs of white drifted from her mouth as she panted, trying to catch her breath. With each step she took, it was as if her angelic powers were being drained away. She stopped and slumped against the damp wall of the cave, unable to take another step. Could she do this? Even if she managed to reach him, would she have any power left to save him?

Gabrielle had warned her it would be like this, but Rachel had dismissed her, especially when she first stepped into Hell. It looked just like home! Lush grass and fragrant flowers lined the landscape as far as she could see. Snowcapped mountains stood as a backdrop against the clear blue skies—even the stream was located in the same exact spot as in Heaven. If it wasn't for the unnerving feeling in the pit of her stomach and the hairs that stood on the back of her neck, she would have sworn she was home.

Considering Lucifer held his captives at the Lake of Fire, she had assumed Hell was a vast empty land of sweltering heat. It wasn't until she found the cave hidden behind a waterfall that she finally understood what Gabrielle meant about not letting her guard down. The cave was frigid. The icy air seemed to seep into her pores and deep into her bones, causing her teeth to chatter uncontrollably.

She wished Gabrielle had given her more information about what to expect. She would've dressed warmer. Gabrielle had only gone once, and she had waited on the outer boundaries of the cave. According to her, one time had been enough. It had taken her days to recover from the experience.

Only Raphael knew what Hell was really like. He had made Gabrielle wait for him while he bravely went through the deepest depths of the cave to reach the lake. He was the only person she knew of who had gone down and returned—alive.

If only she could have asked Raphael about what to expect and how to prepare. She sighed. If she had, there was no way she could've slipped away unnoticed. She would've been reported to Michael and more than likely, would've been put on watch until it was too late.

A sob escaped her at the thought of his death. She slapped a hand over her mouth, horrified as the sound echoed in the darkness, bouncing off the walls. Her body shook as she wrestled with the thought of losing him. She had to pull herself together. If she were caught, it would be the end for both of them.

She took a resolving breath and pushed herself off the wall. *I can do this. I won't lose him.*

Her feet scraped across the floor of the cave as she trudged forward in the darkness. As she rounded a corner, she came up to a pair of tunnels.

*Which way should I go?* Her eyes watered, and she bit down on her lip, frustrated. She was tired. So tired. If she chose the wrong one, she didn't know if she would be able to make it down the second. Time was running out. She had to make a choice, now!

She was about to go down the tunnel to her left when she heard a moan from the right.

*It's him!*

She raced toward the sound with renewed energy, and within minutes, she came into a large cavern. Heat slammed against her body, making her cringe in pain from the abrupt change in temperature. She stopped suddenly, her arms flailing out as she tried to regain her balance and not fall into the molten lava that appeared right before her eyes threatening to singe the tips of her toes.

*The lake!*

Immense heat blurred her vision, and she rubbed her eyes. All she could see was a sea of red heat. *Where is he?*

Searching through the haze, she finally saw a faint figure, motionless. She blinked again and gasped when her eyes finally focused.

*No! It can't be him.*

Across the lake, chained to the wall, naked, was the one person in her life who she couldn't be without. The one person for whom she would defy the orders of the most high of archangels just so she could save him.

Uriel.

Tears spilled down her heated cheeks as she took in his once magnificent body, scorched by the lava that splashed onto his skin. His beautiful downy-white wings were now a grotesque black. With each movement he made, feathers turned to ash and fluttered lifelessly to the ground.

"Uriel," she croaked.

Uriel lifted his head, and pained eyes looked back at her, a startling blue against the black of his charred face. "No," he groaned. "Leave. Leave now. He'll be here—"

The cave rumbled, and lava sprouted into the air. A splattering of the searing liquid fell onto his chest. He arched his back and screeched.

"I'm coming, Uriel!" She tore off her cloak and flicked her wings open.

"It's too late for me," he rasped. "Don't do this."

"No, it's not. I don't care what the others say. You've redeemed yourself. You deserve another chance."

He looked deep into her eyes. "Forgive me. I'm unworthy of you."

"There is nothing to forgive. I love you."

Desperate to find a way to get to him, Rachel looked around the cavern. She swallowed hard as she flit her wings and with all the strength she could muster, propelled herself into the air. She was only able to get herself a couple of feet off the ground. It was as if an invisible barrier was holding her down. Frantically, she looked around for another way to get to him and saw a narrow stone path with lava washing across it. There was no other way to him.

With all her might, she pushed herself upward, trying to get distance from the fiery liquid. The cave shook again, and a wave of lava slammed against the walls, sending droplets of lava flying into the air and onto her wings.

She wailed in pain and began to fall.

"No, Rachel. Go back," Uriel moaned.

Before Rachel could tell him there was no way she was leaving him, she felt a rush of air on her back. An arm wrapped tightly around her waist and yanked her away from the lake, away from Uriel.

"Take her...Gabrielle," Uriel gasped. "Keep her...safe."

"You have my word," Gabrielle said as she tightened her hold on Rachel.

"No!" Rachel screamed, struggling against Gabrielle's steel-like arms. "Let me go. Let. Me. Go!"

Rachel stretched out her arms as if just by doing so, she could hold on to him. "Uriel! Uriel!"

Just as Gabrielle flew out of the cavern, a loud thunderclap rocked the cave, and the sound of his screams ripped through her, mixing with her own.

Then, silence.

*He's gone.*

She fell limply into Gabrielle's arms as they flew back through the frigid tunnel. The cold spread to her face, her hands, and then crept into her heart and the deepest part of her soul until there was nothing left except a dark numbness. It didn't matter. Nothing mattered anymore.

When they flew out of the waterfall and into the sunlight, she stared lifelessly at the clouds drifting overhead. And though the sun shone down on her face, she couldn't feel its warmth. She doubted if she would ever feel it again. The cold emptiness in her heart would be there forever because Uriel was dead.

"Wait! Uri died? Like died, died? No longer existing, died?" Naomi gawked at Rachel and then glanced at Uri. His dimple flashed as he grinned. "But, you're...you're here."

Rachel stared off into the distance with a sad expression as if she were still back in the cave.

"Rachel? Are you okay?" Naomi shook her shoulder, her brow furrowed with worry. She wasn't used to seeing her friend so sad. Out of all the angels she'd met during her short time in Heaven, Rachel was the most cheerful, always chirping away about angel gossip. She wished she hadn't asked Rachel about how she and Uri met. Naomi had no idea about their tragic past or that Rachel and Uri were ever apart. Uri, who had shortened his name from Uriel, was always by Rachel's side.

When Naomi first met Uri, she'd been taken off guard by the way he winked and teased her. And he was a hugger, just like Rachel. She'd thought Lash would be jealous of the way Uri flirted with her. But then she noticed he was that way with everyone, even Gabrielle.

Heaven was not at a loss for drop-dead gorgeous angels. Although Lash's dark, brooding looks were more her type, she had to admit Uri was attractive. His dark blond hair was worn short with long bangs that flopped on his forehead, highlighting teasing blue eyes. His most striking features were his full lips that always seemed to be in a puckered position. Many of the female angels drooled every time Uri kissed their hand "hello" or melted whenever he flashed a smile at them. And if Uri really wanted to get them going, he'd go heavy on his Russian accent.

Despite all the attention he drew, it was clear that his heart belonged to Rachel. Every time she walked into the room, his face would light up and grow even more breathtakingly handsome. It was like all the energy he radiated was because of her.

Rachel blinked a few times, and she shook her head as if bringing herself to the present. "Yeah, sorry. I got lost in memories there for a moment. What were you saying?"

"Ah, my love, allow me to explain to Naomi my miraculous resurrection," Uri said to Rachel.

He leaned over the table and took Naomi's hand into his. He paused and then glanced over at Lash. "May I?"

Lash nodded and leaned back into his seat. "As long as you rein in some of the charm."

Naomi rolled her eyes. "He's just holding my hand. Why *are* you holding my hand, Uri?"

"Tell me, my beautiful Naomi. What do you feel?" Uri gave Rachel a wink.

Naomi blinked, confused. "I, uh, well, I feel your hand."

"Yes, you feel Uri's hand," he said, flipping the "r" as he spoke. "But, who is Uri?"

"What?" She glanced over to Lash, not knowing what to think. He shrugged.

"Is this Uri, flesh and bones?" He slid her hand up his muscular arm. "Or is this Uri?" He then placed her hand over his chiseled chest.

Lash bolted up in his seat. "Hey there, watch it now."

"Shh." Naomi waved a hand. "I think I'm on to something."

"Looks to me like you're feeling Uri up," he mumbled.

Rachel giggled and picked up the cards from the center of the table. "Naomi's right. You're cute when you're jealous."

"I'm not...aw, give me the cards." He snatched the deck from her.

Naomi could feel Lash pouting as he shuffled the cards. She wanted to put his mind at ease, but she was close to figuring out what Uri was trying to explain. It was on the tip of her mind.

"Are you saying that it was only your body that changed?"

Uri grinned. "Very good. This"—he tapped her hand against his chest—"is a new and improved Uri. You like?" He winked.

"Yes."

He beamed, and she heard a muffled giggle from Rachel.

Naomi felt her face grow warm as she pulled her hand off his chest. "I mean...you're a...a...a good friend," she stammered.

She took a breath and tried to re-focus the conversation back to what they were talking about. "So, what you're saying is that the real you, your soul, didn't die. It was still alive."

"She is a smart one, no?" Uri said to Lash.

He grunted.

"Let's take that as a 'yes'." Naomi turned her attention back to the game they were playing. She swiped the pinto beans off the bingo card and looked for another one. Her current one had to be jinxed. She hadn't won one game the entire evening.

She had introduced Mexican bingo to Uri and Rachel a few weeks ago, hoping to have some fun during her time off from training. Rachel loved it so much—probably because she won most of the time—that she and Uri came over every evening to play.

"I learn something new every day. I didn't know it was possible for angels to die, or at least their bodies. It must've been a relief to know Uri was going to come back," Naomi said.

The room went silent.

"Not everyone comes back," Rachel said quietly. Her constant smile disappeared.

"Oh, but *I* did." Uri got up from the table, lifted Rachel from her chair, and placed her on his lap. "It took many years, but I came back to you, my love."

"Three thousand, three hundred eighty-six years, five months, two days, twelve hours, forty-eight minutes, and twenty-three seconds," Rachel said under her breath.

Naomi gasped. He was gone for that long? Her chest tightened as Uri tenderly brushed a tear off Rachel's cheek. If angels could die, then Lash could too, and there was no guarantee he'd be resurrected. All this time, she had thought there was nothing that could tear them apart. She'd thought she had forever with him.

"When did you die?" she asked.

"1400 BC. My return wasn't until...hmm, let's see, 1967 or so, when I was born into a human body. Not too much different than when you were born into your human body."

"Only he was in Chernobyl instead of Texas," Rachel poked Uri in the chest. "I finally saw him again when he turned nineteen."

"Chernobyl in the '80s," Lash sighed. "I remember that."

"Yeah, me too," Rachel said. "I'd never been so happy and frustrated in my life. Believe me, Lash, I totally understand what you went through when you were assigned to Naomi."

"Uri came back human?" Naomi turned to him. "You didn't know you were an angel before?"

"Nope. It took much convincing from Rachel. Unlike you, I was not the most, umm, should I say, moral of humans." Uri winked at her. "Of course, Rachel changed all that for me, and we were finally together again."

"But three *thousand* years. I could never..." She looked over at Lash and took a deep calming breath. "I can't even imagine."

"Hey," Lash leaned over and kissed her cheek. "Everything's okay. I'm here," he said as if he could read her thoughts and her fears about living a life without him. How had Rachel done it? All those years without Uri, watching him die the way he did, not knowing if he'd ever come back.

"Why didn't you tell me?"

"It didn't come up." He took the bingo card out of her hand and held her hands in his. "You don't have anything to worry about. Uri's situation is totally unusual. No offense, Uri."

"None taken, my friend," Uri said. "Naomi, Lash is not the most rebellious angel here, as much as he likes to pretend that he is." He grinned, dimples flashing. "There are much worse things one can do than throw a few temper tantrums and mess up assignments."

Lash scowled. "I wouldn't call them tantrums."

"What did you do?" Naomi couldn't imagine Uri doing anything so bad that his punishment was death in Hell. He didn't seem the type. "I didn't know angels could be punished like that."

"It wasn't the archangels who punished him." Rachel looked down at Uri's bingo card, frowned, and reached over to the table to get another. "They would never do that."

"Oh, I can see Gabrielle ordering something like that," Lash said.

"Lash," Naomi warned. Gabrielle was still a sore spot for him. Rachel had told her how Gabrielle and Lash didn't get along. So, when Gabrielle was assigned to be her supervisor, she thought Gabrielle would be difficult to work with. Instead, she was very patient with Naomi and even gave her extra time to complete some of her training. She did notice that Gabrielle was all business and never interacted with any of the angels on a personal level. Naomi could understand that. It must be difficult for her to be second in command next to Michael. She hadn't met him yet, but everyone spoke about him with high reverence, including Lash. The only time Gabrielle appeared to let her guard down was when she was with Raphael. If she didn't know any better, she could swear Gabrielle was in love with him.

"What?" Lash looked innocently at her. "It's true. If it were me, she'd do it in a heartbeat."

"Gabrielle can be a bit...stiff at times, but she means well." Rachel's big brown eyes glistened with tears as she looked into the distance, appearing to remember something. "She risked her life, coming after me, and she didn't have to tell me how to get to the Lake of Fire."

"Uh, huh," Lash looked at her skeptically for a moment, then turned his attention to Uri. "So, what *did* you do?"

"You don't know?" Naomi asked, surprised. She figured since Rachel and Lash were such good friends, they would've talked about it by now.

"Lash knows I was killed and then was brought back. I just haven't told anyone why," Uri said, appearing flustered. He looked at Rachel nervously before he continued. "You see, I was a very different person back then. In 1400 BC, I went to the City of Ai with Raphael and Luci—"

"Oh, they don't want to know about the boring stuff." Rachel jumped off his lap. She rifled through the stack of bingo cards in the center of the table and looked closely at each one, avoiding eye contact as she spoke. "Uri was held captive by Lucifer and Saleos. And due to, uh, special circumstances, the archangels decided to, uh, let him"—she sank to her seat and swallowed—"die."

"That's cruel." Naomi couldn't imagine what he'd done that was so bad to have him and Rachel deserve to suffer like that. She eyed Rachel carefully, and she squirmed under her scrutiny. There was something she wasn't telling her. Other than Lash, Rachel had grown to be one of her closest friends, like a sister, sharing everything with her—until now.

"The City of Ai," Lash said. "That sounds familiar. Where have I heard of that before?"

Naomi was caught by surprise at Rachel's forced, high-pitched giggle. "Look at this card, Naomi. La Muerte," she read and then handed her the card with a picture of a skeleton holding a scythe. "It doesn't look at all like Jeremy. It's missing his new crocodile boots. Isn't that right, Uri?"

Uri furrowed his brow, confused, then as if picking up on Rachel's cue said, "Yes, his boots. Very nice."

Naomi saw Lash stiffen and pause mid-shuffle at the mention of Jeremy's name. Jeremy had disappeared the day after she was reunited with Lash. She had heard about the fight Lash had with him and felt awful about it. She had asked Raphael about Jeremy, hoping she could do something to help reunite the two best friends. Raphael had merely shaken his head sadly and said Gabrielle had sent him on an extended assignment and that he didn't know when he would return.

"So, Jeremy's back." Lash resumed shuffling the cards, his voice strained.

Rachel gazed at Lash and then Naomi, her eyes filled with pity. She then turned to Lash with what looked like a forced smile. "I saw him this morning. Maybe you, Jeremy, and Uri could start up your poker games again."

Lash's jaw tensed. He stared down at the cards as his thumbs flipped through them. He tapped the deck against the table and shuffled again without a word.

The room grew uncomfortable as he avoided answering the question.

"That's a great idea," Naomi said, forcing her voice to sound cheerful. She glanced at Rachel and Uri, noticed the knowing looks they were giving each other, and sighed.

More secrets. What was it with this place and all the secrets? She wasn't used to having people keeping things from her, especially after Lash finally revealed that he was a seraph and Raphael had told her she was the seventh archangel.

Lash had even told her about his conversation with Raphael and how Rebecca, her grandmother's guardian angel, was his mother and Raphael his father. And when he told her Jeremy was his older brother, she had thought they were done with secrets...apparently not. How frustrating! No wonder Lash was moody when she first met him. She didn't blame him one bit.

"Explain it to me again: why do we have to use pinto beans?" Lash asked as he grabbed a handful.

He was obviously trying to change the subject. She sighed. Maybe it was better to stick to playing Mexican bingo.

"We don't have to use beans. Bingo chips would work just as well. Welita...Welita liked to use beans." A familiar pang rung through her chest, the same one she felt whenever she thought of her grandmother and her cousin, Chuy.

When Naomi had first arrived in Heaven, she had checked in on them during breaks from her training. But each time she had, it had become harder and harder for her to tear herself away from the bridge over the stream, the only window she had to their world. Gabrielle had picked up on her inability to concentrate after each of her visits and ordered her to avoid the bridge until after her training was complete.

At first, she was appalled that Gabrielle was basically asking her to forget about her family. Lash, of course, was outraged and offered to bring it up to Michael, claiming she was working hard and checking in on her family helped to ease the transition to Heaven. After she had calmed down, she realized Gabrielle was right. Her new life and family were here with him, and the best way she could adjust was to delve into her new role as archangel.

"Naomi," Lash gently touched her shoulder. "Are you okay?"

"Yeah, I was just thinking about Welita. I miss her and Chuy."

"I miss them too...and Bear," Lash said about her grandmother's Chihuahua. "Crazy little fur ball."

Naomi wondered what they were doing at that moment. She wondered if it was late in the evening there like it was up in Heaven. What time zone was Heaven in?

Chuy and his best friend, Lalo, were probably sitting around the dinner table right now, just having gotten off work. Chuy would be on his second helping and Lalo on his third. Lalo was like a member of the family, and even he called her grandmother "Welita" rather than her given name Anita.

Naomi could actually see, in her mind, Lalo sneaking pieces of Welita's chicken mole to Bear, while Welita was busy cleaning the kitchen.

Rachel gave a loud yawn as she stood up, scraping the chair across the floor. "I'm pooped. Come on, Uri. Let's go home. Why don't we play at our place tomorrow?"

"You don't have to leave," Naomi said.

Rachel went to her and gave her a hug. "I know that. You and Lash should have some alone time together. You've been working so hard lately. Besides, Uri says he has a special treat for me tonight."

"Every night is special with you." Uri swept her into his arms and flicked out his wings.

"Uri!" Rachel squealed. "What are you doing? I have wings too, you know."

Uri walked around the table, headed to the living room, where a wall of windows overlooked the valley. All the windows were open, letting in a cool breeze.

"Lash, you're smart moving out of the commune and into your own home." He stepped to the edge of the center window and looked down. "The view from up here is magnificent. But why so far away from everybody?"

As much as Naomi loved living with Lash, it had been crowded in his small room. Lash had immediately rectified the situation by building a small cottage on the ridge of a mountain that overlooked the angels' living quarters. More importantly, she could see the bridge from their home, a reminder that Welita was only minutes away. She loved it. But, in the back of her mind, she wondered if there was another reason why he wanted to live away from the others—or maybe one person in particular.

Lash wrapped his arms around Naomi and kissed her neck. "Oh, let's just say we wanted a little privacy." His hot breath hit against her ear as he whispered, "And space for extracurricular activities."

## 2

Jeremy leaned against the railing of the bridge, sapphire eyes gazing in the direction of the mountain. In the distance, he could see the twinkling of lights on the highest peak.

He closed his eyes for a moment, waiting for the ache to pass. Being away for the past few weeks, he hadn't even realized it was still there, lingering deep in his heart. He had Gabrielle to thank for that. How did she know what he was feeling when he couldn't understand it himself?

He'd thought spending time away from Lash and Naomi would help him get some perspective on what he was feeling. But when he returned and stood alone in Lash's empty room, he questioned who his heart was aching for—Lash or Naomi.

His hands scrubbed over his face with frustration. He had let himself go since he left, almost as if punishing himself. He didn't bother with shaving. He didn't even bother dressing in his favorite custom suits anymore. Instead, he wore whatever he could throw on, like black slacks and T-shirts. Even his once perfectly coiffed hair was different, with scraggly bangs falling over his eyes and the rest long enough to brush against his collarbone. The only luxury he allowed himself was a black leather jacket that matched his new crocodile boots.

He looked up into the darkening sky, trying to pinpoint the exact moment when everything changed. When had he turned from a loyal best friend to someone who was not to be trusted? Could he blame Lash for not having faith in him when even he didn't know if he could trust himself when it came to Naomi?

Jeremy pushed himself off the rail and paced the length of the bridge, his shiny black boots clicking on the wood. *I was doing my job. That's all.*

Watching over Lash and making sure he took Naomi to Shiprock—that was what he'd been told to do, and he had done it. He'd followed his orders to a "T." So what if he may have checked in on them a little more than what was required of him? There was no harm in that. And he may have felt a little bit of jealousy—no, concern. Yes, that was it; he was concerned when he saw the obvious attraction between the two of them. He had to warn Lash to leave her alone. He'd thought it would ruin Lash's chance to return home.

Jeremy froze as he recalled the words he had said to Lash.

*She's not for you.*

Why had he said that to him?

*You know why,* a small voice whispered in his head.

He slammed his hand against the rail. He knew perfectly well why. He wished he could forget all of it and just have a fresh start with Lash and Naomi. But he couldn't.

Fighting against his memories of her, he gripped the railing so hard his knuckles went white. It had been easier before, when his sole focus was accomplishing a mission. Now, he struggled to push from his mind how he felt when he first saw her: long, dark hair falling forward draping her beautiful face as she hovered over a dying Deborah. It had been as if lightning hit his chest and restarted a heart that he hadn't known had stopped. It had only been when Lash appeared obviously threatened by the way he looked at her that he'd been able to pull himself away and focus on the task at hand. Ever since then, he'd been shaking away growing feelings, feelings he'd had no idea where they came from until Raphael had told him—he was his son, and long ago he had been betrothed to Naomi.

"Are you ready?"

Jeremy whipped around at the sound of the voice. "Gabrielle. I thought I was alone."

She stepped from out of the shadows. A breeze blew soft blonde waves around a stern face. "You've been in isolation for weeks. Have you prepared yourself for your new task?"

Jeremy was surprised by her tone. Was he dreaming that only a few weeks ago, it had been Gabrielle who suggested he leave to get some space from all that had happened between him and Lash? She had seemed so kind and patient.

He looked back up at the mountain and wondered if Lash was still angry with him, and as much as he tried not to, he thought of Naomi. "Couldn't this be given to Lash? He's better suited."

"Michael was adamant that this assignment be overseen by you. Besides, you have your own assignment to attend to on Earth." Her voice was firm as she eyed him carefully. She must have seen something on his face because her face softened. It was the same look she'd given him after his fight with Lash. "Did the time away not help you to prepare?"

"Gabrielle, can't you make an exception? I've always done my duty, and I've never questioned you or Michael for any of the assignments you two have given me...even when you asked me to strike down my best friend."

"It is because of your loyal service all these years that you have risen through the ranks to become an archangel," she pointed out. "You know that with this role comes greater responsibility. If Lash had been as obedient as you...well, never mind that. He's hopeless."

"Why do you hate him?"

Gabrielle arched an eyebrow. "I am merely stating what is true. Have his past behaviors not proven that?"

Jeremy shook his head. He couldn't understand the animosity she had towards Lash. He'd thought once Lash had finally proven himself that she'd be more lenient with him. He'd returned only to find that she was exactly the same as when he left.

"If you're worried about Lash, I assure you, there won't be any interference from him. I'll see to that."

"Worried? You could say that. When he finds out that I'm the one to be paired with the love his life on her first assignment, Hell—"

She glared at his choice of words.

"Uh, what I mean is"—he cleared his throat—"you know, he's not the most reasonable of angels. And we did leave things hanging there after our fight."

"I had suggested you take the time off in order to give you, and hopefully Lash, space to reflect on all that has transpired." Gabrielle glanced up at the mountain and then back to Jeremy. "And maybe resolve any feelings that may be…lingering."

Jeremy swallowed nervously at her innuendo. "I'm not sure what you mean."

Her voice was low and soft as she spoke. "You do realize you have a reputation for being a great poker player. Your skills would be useful in this situation, don't you think?"

He furrowed his brow. "I don't understand."

Gabrielle sighed. "Although I abhor the game, I am quite skilled at maintaining what you call a poker face. I would say I've been quite successful at it."

Her face changed as if a mask was taken off, and the tough demeanor she was notorious for was replaced by a soft and vulnerable woman. "You have feelings for the girl. It was clear when you were by her bedside, waiting for her to awake. In fact, it was written all over your face the first time you saw her when you were on assignment with Deborah and Nathan."

"You saw that?"

"Yes." Her voice was soft.

"Why? Why were you watching over me?"

"Because I knew how you felt about her long ago when she was to become your wife. And I know feelings like that don't disappear—even when memories are suppressed."

He took a step forward and gripped her arm. "What do you know? Tell me." He needed to know more. Maybe if he knew what happened in his past, he could get rid of his growing feelings.

She winced and looked down at his hand.

"Sorry." He dropped his hand. He was going too far. He needed to get himself under control.

"It's not my story to tell." She rubbed the spot on her arm where he had grabbed her. "That is something Raphael wants to share with you, Lash, and Naomi. He is with Michael as we speak, seeking permission to disclose some of your past."

"Will we get our memories back?"

"It's unlikely. I'm sure Raphael has shared with you that the suppression of your memory is part of his punishment."

Jeremy nodded. While he was waiting by Naomi's side for her to wake up, Raphael had told him why he and Lash couldn't remember their past. "It seems like a long time to be punished."

"It is not for you to decide how long a punishment should be," she reprimanded. "But I agree. I believe this has continued because it is all tied together with what is happening now, including your current assignment. What Raphael did had a ripple effect not only for you, Lash, and Naomi, but ultimately with..." she paused as Jeremy stared at her with bated breath.

"Well, I must take my leave. I just wanted to tell you that your assignment will come soon, and I wanted to give you time to prepare yourself."

Jeremy let out a breath, disappointed. She wasn't giving away anything. Regardless, he had to figure out a way to get out of this assignment if he ever wanted to make things right with Lash.

"Is there any way I can appeal my assignment? Perhaps if I speak to Michael?"

"You could, but it will only anger him more. I have already spoken to him on your behalf. How do you think you were given permission to leave and place yourself in isolation?"

"You did that?"

"Yes. Why do you look so surprised? I've been known to do a nice thing or two from time to time," she said with a twinkle in her green eyes.

He blinked with shock. She actually looked like she was teasing.

"Michael wanted you to be in charge of her instruction as well as pair with her on her first assignment. I convinced him to allow me to do the training."

"Gabrielle, I don't know how to thank you." If only she could be this gracious with Lash, life would be so different for his brother. Although Lash would never admit it, all he ever wanted from her was respect.

"There you are. I have been searching for you, Jeremiel." Raphael called from the direction of the gardens. An older replica of himself walked toward them with a large smile on his face. "Welcome back, my son."

Jeremy swallowed thickly at those words. Raphael had always felt like a father to him. Although he'd always seemed to lavish his attention on Lash, Raphael managed to spend some of his time with him.

"Based on the smile on your face, I take it your meeting with Michael went well," Gabrielle said.

"Yes. Yes, it did. He agreed it would benefit us all to divulge some information about our past in the hopes of strengthening our connections and promoting healing." Raphael turned to Jeremy and slapped him on the shoulder. "Come, Jeremiel. We have much to share with your brother."

Just before Jeremy turned, he caught Gabrielle looking at Raphael with such longing that he did a double take. Her green eyes narrowed, and her face shifted back into the old Gabrielle, and he wondered if he was imaging things.

She glanced up at the mountain and back at him, giving him a subtle smile. "Remember what I said, Jeremy. Play your game of poker."

# 3

Naomi placed the dishes in the sink and feverishly cleaned the kitchen, trying to erase the image of a dying Uri out of her mind. She didn't want to think about the possibility of losing Lash like that.

"What are you doing?" Lash stood behind her, trailing a finger down her neck.

"Cleaning." She swept the beans into a container and placed the bingo cards in a small box.

"I meant what I said." He took the box from her hands and placed it back on the table.

Smoldering hazel eyes locked with hers and slowly drifted down to her mouth. He gently stroked a thumb across her lower lip and stared at it, mesmerized.

Her breath hitched, and she inhaled his delicious scent, making her forget about Uri, Rachel, Hell, and death. "What did you say?"

He leaned in closer, his lips hovering above hers, feather light as they brushed against hers, whispering, "You know."

He lifted his head and gave her a sexy smirk that never failed to make her body seem like it was on fire. Long fingers wove through her hair. He lifted a thick wavy strand to his nose and inhaled. His chest rumbled with pleasure, making her weak in the knees.

Gently, he swept her hair to her other shoulder, keeping his eyes locked with hers. His fingers curled around the nape of her neck, and he pulled her to him.

She quivered as his tongue swirled around the shell of her ear, hot and wet. She let out a soft moan.

"Am I distracting you?" His voice was deep and sensuous.

"N-no." She gasped as searing lips pressed against her neck and worked their way down. "You said...something about...activities?"

He lifted her hand and placed it on his chest. She could feel the searing heat of his toned body under his shirt. "Mm-hmm." His chest rumbled, making her hand tingle.

Pressing his hand over hers, his eyes lit up teasingly. "You like the new and improved Lash?"

He guided her hand down his chest, and she delighted in the feel of his hardened muscles. "Yes," she breathed as her fingers lined the crevices of his abs. "More than you know."

"Show me." His voice was rough with desire.

Twining fingers into his silky soft hair, she pulled him down to her. Feverish lips crashed down onto hers. Hot wet lips devoured her mouth; his chin scraped across hers with each plunge of his tongue, leaving her chin pink and raw.

She tugged on his shirt, desperate to feel his skin and the warmth of his chest against hers. They separated for a moment as clothing was tossed on the floor. Then Lash reached down and lifted her up, and she wrapped her legs tightly around his waist.

She felt her back against the cool wall as Lash pressed himself against her. She moaned at the hardness of his touch, and she throbbed, wanting him, needing him. They could do this a thousand times, and it still wouldn't be enough.

She clawed at his back as his lips swept down her throat and over the top of her full breasts. She tilted her head back, moaning and squeezing her legs tighter. Lash groaned.

She ran her tongue over his strong square jaw, relishing the scratchy feel of his stubble. He moaned again, and she gasped as he grew unbelievably harder under her.

Before she knew it, there was a loud clatter of table and chairs falling to the ground as Lash crashed out of the kitchen and into their bedroom, holding her tightly against him.

When he released her, she fell back into a cloud of softness. Lash stood over her, his eyes simmering with passion. "You're so beautiful."

Slowly, he lay down beside her, his fingers ghosting over her lips, down her neck and circling her breast. She moaned at his feather-light touch.

"Come here." She pulled him to her.

His rock-hard body pressed against her chest as he kissed her deeply.

"Naomi, my Naomi," he mumbled as he sucked on her neck, tasting her. "I love you."

Her heart swelled with love for him. She'd never grow tired of hearing those words.

"You are mine. Forever," he whispered.

A sudden nagging feeling swept through her as the word forever echoed in her mind. Then she saw an image of Rachel's grief-stricken face.

"Wait, Lash," she said, sitting up in bed. "I just thought of something."

"I'll clean the mess in the kitchen later." He pulled her back down to him and in between his kisses said, "Less thinking, more doing."

She sat back up again. Something about this was off. But what? She hadn't had this strange feeling before. Why now? "Something's wrong."

He groaned and flipped over on his back. "What could be wrong? We're alone; we're together."

"It's not that."

"What is it then?"

"Should we be together?"

He shot up, his face looking terrified. "Are you having doubts about us?"

"No, no! Not at all." She immediately felt guilty for making him think that. "That's not what I meant. You're the only one for me. I can't ever be without you." She leaned over and kissed him deeply.

He sighed with relief. "What's wrong then?"

"I just meant, should we be doing, you know, this?" Naomi pointed to his naked, his *gloriously* naked, body.

He pulled her to him and nuzzled her neck. "Mmm. Definitely."

Naomi quivered as his hands stroked her breasts. She fell back into the bed. Yes, this was right. It felt so right. What was she thinking?

Her hands stroked his chest. He felt so good.

"God, Naomi. I want you so much."

*God!*

"Wait, Lash," she panted, trying to catch her breath. Slowly, memories of long afternoons in catechism classes and Welita's lectures on chastity resurfaced. "I mean should we be together like this, since we're not married?"

He pulled back and looked at her, stunned. "Married?"

She bit down on her lip, not sure how to broach the subject. It wasn't like she was a prude or anything like that. Lash wasn't her first. The thought of having sex before marriage never bothered her before, despite Welita's and her father's lectures about staying chaste. But things were different now. She was an archangel. Wasn't she supposed to be a role model or something like that?

"Well, I don't know if angels get married or have some kind of formal union. I mean, I don't know if things like marriage mean the same thing here as they do on Earth."

His lips curled into a smile. "They do. Many angel couples make vows of commitment to each other, Uri and Rachel for one." He tucked a strand of hair behind her ear. "Is that what you want?"

She looked deep into his eyes. "Yes. I want to be bound to you, forever."

He cupped her face. His eyes were filled with so much love, it took her breath away. "There's nothing I want more than to be bound to you too. I'll talk to Michael tomorrow and make the arrangements." He then leaned over and kissed her.

Slowly, she felt herself falling back into the bed, and his hands caressed her inner thighs.

She moaned, and the guilty feeling resurfaced again. "Lash, maybe we should wait until its official."

He groaned and flipped on his back again. "You're killing me, Naomi."

"I'm sorry. It's just, well, maybe it would be better if we did this the right way."

"Why now? We've been doing this nonstop since you got here." He sat up and gave her a smoldering look. "And if I recall, your loud enthusiasm was one of the reasons why I built our home up on the side of this mountain far away from prying eyes and ears. I think you may have even busted Gabrielle's ear drums, based on the dirty looks she's been giving me lately."

Her jaw dropped, and her face grew hot. Besides having enhanced sight and strength, angels also had amplified hearing. Most of the time, that was seen as a positive. But when you were living in close quarters and wanted privacy? Not so much.

"I ... you... well..." She was so embarrassed.

He chuckled and kissed the tip of her nose. "You're so cute when you're flustered."

"Argh!" She got out of bed and put on a robe. "I'm being serious."

He leaned back against the headboard, his arms behind his head. "Tell me: what's the real problem?"

She sat on the edge of the bed. He read her like an open book. "It's what Rachel said about her and Uri. I don't want that to happen to us."

His eyes grew serious, and he reached out to stroke her cheek. "It won't. I'm here with you. I'm not going anywhere."

"But what if we get in trouble for doing this premarital sex stuff? I don't want to take any chances."

"Naomi, that's not going to happen."

"It'll make me feel better if we make it official." She leaned over and kissed him gently.

He looked at her and shook his head, laughing. "If it will really make you feel better..."

"Yes, it well." She beamed. "Tell me what the ceremony is like."

"Well, it's not too different from the way you're probably used to seeing. Michael performs a binding ceremony, and the couple makes vows of commitment to each other in front of witnesses.

"Have you been to one before?"

"Uri and Rachel had their ceremony a while back. It was 1987 or '88. I'm not sure. It was definitely the 80s, though. He had this weird Flock of Seagulls hair thing going on back then."

She laughed at the vision of Uri with his hair styled like a pair of wings to match the wings on his back. The style was all the rage back in the 80s. Her father's love for alternative music and new wave bands introduced her to a wide range of strange looking hair and fashion. "Yeah, I can definitely see him doing that."

Naomi's laughter quieted, and she became somber again as she thought about the ceremony. She'd never seen herself being married or committed to anyone, not until she met Lash. She knew it was something Welita would have loved to see. And her father, he would've loved to walk her down the aisle with her arm in his. Tears pricked her eyes at the thought that her family wouldn't be there to see it.

"I thought you were happy about this?" His voice was soft.

She looked up at him and forced a smile on her face. "I am. I'm committing myself to you." She kissed his lips gently.

"Be honest. We don't want to start our forever with secrets, do we?"

She sighed. "It's just that I miss my family sometimes. They won't be here to see this. And my dad, I'll never get to experience this with him."

Her eyes widened with surprise as his face paled. Without a word, he quickly got out of bed, went to the kitchen, and poured himself a glass of water.

She watched his back muscles tense as he faced away from her, silent. "Lash?"

He downed his drink before turning his attention back to her. His lips were wet as he spoke. "I wish there was something I could do to fix that for you."

"Oh, Lash. It isn't your fault my father is gone or that I'm here. I just need to keep reminding myself that by being here, I can take care of my family better."

"Uh, Naomi." He brushed the moisture off his lips with the back of his hand. "There's something I need to tell you about that."

"What is it?"

He licked his lips nervously and opened his mouth, about to say something, then closed it.

"Lash?" She felt panic set in. Something was wrong. Why was he acting so strange?

He shook his head and then looked at her with a smile that didn't quite reach his eyes. "You're absolutely right. Together, we can watch over Welita and the others. Tell you what: let's take a peek at them in the morning."

"I'd love that!" She beamed and then suddenly frowned. "No, wait. I don't think we should. Gabrielle was pretty firm about me staying away from the bridge for a while."

"Ah, don't mind her. We'll be real quick about it."

She struggled between wanting to follow Gabrielle's orders and seeing Welita. She wanted so badly to tell her about her binding ceremony to Lash. It was the closest thing she had next to Welita being there. "Maybe I should go alone."

"I want to go with you."

"I don't want you to get in trouble. You just got back!"

"Will you stop worrying? I'll be fine. Besides, *I* wasn't told to stay away from the bridge." He grinned. "I'd love to see them. They'll be my family too real soon."

She threw her arms around him. "Lash, you've made me the happiest woman in the world. I love you."

He pulled back, searching her eyes. "No matter what?"

She blinked with surprise. "Of course. Why would you ask a silly question like—"

She jumped at the sudden pounding on the door. "Who could that be? The only people who come over are Uri and Rachel." Naomi cinched her robe tighter as she padded toward the door.

He grabbed her hand. "Don't."

She laughed. "What's wrong with you today? You're so jumpy."

"I'll get it," he said.

She shook her head as he frantically threw on a pair of jeans. "You act like we live in the middle of the most dangerous neighborhood in Houston."

He ran to the front door and swung it open. His jaw tensed and his hands curled into fists.

"Bro!" Jeremy cried as he stepped inside, slapping him on the back as he passed him. "Am I too late for bingo?"

# 4

A tumult of emotions ran through Lash as he watched Jeremy step into the room. He took a deep breath, reminding himself that this was his brother, his longtime best friend. He tried his best to shake the vision, no, the *memory* he had of Jeremy and Naomi.

It was a memory that kept replaying in his head, even after Jeremy left on his so-called break and Lash moved Naomi up to their mountain home. It was of Jeremy handing a wedding band to Naomi's father, a symbol of the old days, when the first-born of the household made his intentions for marriage directly to the woman's father. Raphael hadn't denied it was a memory.

And Jeremy? He didn't have to say anything—the look on his face said it all. Lash remembered the expression on his face when he first laid his eyes on Naomi. Lash couldn't shake that look from his mind. Now there he was, acting as if nothing had changed.

Even though Naomi was adamant that all her memories were of him, he couldn't help but wonder if in the past, a past she couldn't remember, she had loved Jeremy. Would that change now that Jeremy was back and she got to know him better? It seemed like everyone loved him, even Gabrielle.

No. He had to believe Naomi would stay true to him, no matter what.

Just as he was about to speak, Raphael floated through the door, his smile disappearing when he took in the expression on Lash's face.

"Have we come at a bad time?"

*You could say that,* Lash thought. His eyes followed Jeremy as the golden-haired angel walked toward the one person he wanted to keep all to himself. When Naomi smiled up at him, he fought the instinct to grab her and take her as far away from his brother as possible.

"Of course not," Naomi said to him and then turned to Jeremy. "So, spill it."

Jeremy paled, and an odd expression flashed across his face. "Uh, spill what?"

"The boots. Rachel said you got a pair," she said, looking down expectantly at his feet.

Jeremy let out a rush of air, and the ever-present grin returned. "You bet!" He stuck out his foot. "Tell me these boots don't rock it."

She laughed. "You definitely made some changes while you were gone. I miss your suits, though I love the leather jacket. Is that why you disappeared for so long? Shopping?"

"Why? Miss me?" Jeremy winked.

Lash took a step forward. He didn't like where this was going—not at all.

Raphael immediately stepped in front of Lash, blocking his way. "We all missed you, Jeremiel," he said.

"You left so quickly the day after you and Lash…" Naomi bit her lip and glanced nervously at Lash. "Well, I was hoping you two would talk it out."

"That is why we are here," Raphael said. "I was given permission to divulge some information to you about our past. Shall we have a seat?"

As they gathered in the living room, Lash firmly placed Naomi's hand in his. He eyed Jeremy, who sat across from them with Raphael. There was something off about Jeremy. Although he was smiling, he didn't seem happy. The special spark that drew everyone to him was gone. In all the years he'd known him, Jeremy had never looked like he did now. It had always been the other way around, where he was the brooding one and Jeremy was by his side, distracting him from whatever troubled him. He struggled between his desire to console his old friend and wanting to stay angry with him.

He watched Jeremy's eyes zoom in on Naomi's hand as it held on to his, and then quickly look away when Lash caught him staring.

*It's easier to stay mad,* he thought.

"Before Jeremiel left on his"—Raphael glanced at Jeremy and cleared his throat—"extended assignment, I shared with him the information that I had shared with you, Lahash."

"Hermano!" Jeremy held out a fist toward him, grinning. "Don't leave me hanging, Bro."

Lash felt Naomi jabbing him in the ribs. *How did she get such a pointy elbow?*

He sighed and reached out to fist-bump him.

Naomi beamed. "That would explain why you two were such great friends all those years."

"Were," Lash mumbled under his breath.

Jeremy frowned slightly as he sat back in his seat. "You know I would've told you about my assignment if I were allowed."

"Yeah, sure. Whatever."

"Lash," Naomi reprimanded.

He let go of her hand, scowling. "I thought you didn't trust him, and now you're all 'let's be one happy family.' I don't know. Maybe I'm better off not remembering the past."

"How can not having a memory of your own family be better? It's a part of who you are," she said.

"Those are wise words, Naomi," Raphael said, his voice low and with authority. He turned to Lash and looked him straight in the eye. "The person you are today is made from who you were yesterday. Your past influences the present, and it is family that shapes your growth."

"See, that's exactly what I mean. We all know I'm a screw-up." Lash stood up and paced the floor. "I only had a few memories shown to me, but they were enough for me to know, to realize that even back then, I was second best—to you." He directed at Jeremy.

"Lahash," Raphael stood up and placed a hand on his shoulder. "Lucifer showed you only what serves to benefit him."

Lash pulled away. "No, Raphael. It was more than that. Even before the memories, I felt it. I know you were disappointed with me staying a seraph and getting disciplined after almost every assignment. Jeremy and I both started as seraphs, and within the year he was assigned the position of archangel. And me, well..."

"Be fair, Lash," Jeremy said. "You antagonized Gabrielle even from the beginning."

Lash spun around. "You, shut up!"

Naomi gasped. "Lash!"

"No, Naomi. You weren't there, and you don't know." He breathed hard. He was tired of everyone taking Jeremy's side. "At the time, I didn't see it. But now I do. I was questioned every step of the way. And Jeremy? Never. We did the same things, but Jeremy was always let off, and me? I'm the one who got in trouble. It was as if he could do no wrong."

"That's not true!" Jeremy jumped to his feet.

"You may be right," Raphael said softly.

Jeremy froze, and Lash's jaw dropped.

The room was a tense silence for a moment before Raphael continued. "Please sit down and let me explain."

Naomi tugged Lash's arm. He took one look at the tears glistening in her eyes, and he melted. He hadn't meant to get mad at her. "I'm sorry. Forgive me?"

She nodded.

Sitting by her side, he placed an arm around her and turned his attention back to Raphael.

"As you know, Jeremiel is your older brother. As was the custom at the time, the first-born was given rights above all others in the family. He was the heir to what our family owned. With his right as first born, he was to marry before Lahash, and that is where your family came into play," he said looking to Naomi.

She pressed a hand to her chest. "My family?"

"Naomi," Raphael reached over and placed her hand in his. "Your first family is from the City of Ai. Your father owned an inn and was a very successful businessman. He was considered to be an esteemed leader of the city." He released her hand and looked to Jeremy and Lash. "You two were born of a human mother and an angelic father."

"Rebecca," Lash said.

Raphael nodded, and his face grew sad at the sound of the name.

"So, we're Nephilim," Jeremy said, sitting back down.

"What?" Naomi gasped. "Aren't the Nephilim evil giants?"

"Some of the stories that have been told over the years are not entirely accurate," Raphael said. "Just as there are evil people, there were Nephilim who took advantage of their heritage. As for my sons, I taught them humility and respect for all those around them. And, at the time, they did not know they were born half-angels."

"I thought all the Nephilim were wiped out?" Naomi asked.

Raphael smiled. "You know your scripture very well."

"Catechism classes every Wednesday. I skipped once, but Chuy ratted me out to Welita. I couldn't sit down for a week." Naomi sighed with a smile on her face, as if remembering.

Raphael took a deep breath as if what he was going to say next was difficult. "Among the humans, the Nephilim stood out for their beauty and strength. Many people in the city worshipped them as if they were gods. Jeremiel"— he threw a wary glance at Lash—"was favored above all, both human and Nephilim, for his skill and strength. There were many families who desired to betroth their daughters to him, including your family, Naomi."

"That figures," Lash mumbled.

Naomi patted his leg. "It's all in the past. I'm here with you now."

Looking up at her, Lash brushed his finger across her cheek. "Yes, you are." He turned back to Raphael and saw a strange expression on Jeremy's face again. He ignored it, not wanting to upset Naomi again.

"It was not that you were unskilled or lacked strength, my son. I fear I may have encouraged the people's attention directed at Jeremiel and away from you. From the day you two met, it was clear Naomi wanted only you. And I"—he swallowed thickly—"I did everything I could to turn Naomi away from you."

He looked at Lash with tormented eyes. "That is a memory I wish I could forget. Believe me when I tell you, Lahash, there is not a day that goes by when I have not regretted my actions."

"Why would you do such a thing?" Naomi said, her voice sounded raw with ache. "Why would you have wanted to hurt your own son like that?"

Raphael threw a glance at Jeremy and then turned to her. "Because I...I favored Jeremiel." He paused, his eyes fixated on the floor, the words coming slowly, carefully. "And he favored...you."

Lash jumped up and screamed at Jeremy. "Get out!"

"Come on, Lash," Jeremy said in a soft voice, looking up at him. "That was a long time ago."

Lash took a menacing step toward him and looked down at the golden angel who threated to take everyone he loved away from him. He'd done it in the past. What was to stop him from doing it again? "You've been acting strange ever since you set foot in this house. Why is that?"

Jeremy swallowed. "We didn't exactly leave off on good terms the last time we saw each other. I wasn't sure what to expect."

His eyes stared intently at Lash as if he were struggling to convince him.

Lash searched his face, trying to read him. Jeremy was wearing his poker face. *Damn it! He's hiding something.*

"What aren't you telling me?"

"Please, Lash. This doesn't matter anymore." Naomi's soft hands touched his tense arm and turned him around to face her. "For the entire time you've known Jeremy, that you can remember, has he ever tried to take anything away from you?"

"Yes. He let you die. He could've saved you."

"That was different. His job was to bring me here. When I first met him, you told me he was your friend. And if you remember, I wanted to take a tire iron to him."

Lash grinned. "Those were good times."

Naomi looked at him expectantly.

He sighed. "Oh, all right. No, Jeremy never took anything from me."

"And?"

"And, he was always up front with me."

"So, why would you expect anything to be different now?"

She was making too much sense, and he didn't like it. Memories or not, he just couldn't shake off the feeling that Jeremy still wanted her. He gazed into Naomi's pale blue eyes framed by thick black lashes. She was so beautiful. How could he blame any man or angel for wanting her?

"You're right. I guess I'm just being paranoid."

She pecked his cheek with a kiss and then turned to Raphael. "I don't remember any of this, and what little flashes of memory that have resurfaced have always been of Lash, and now I understand why. I love him and nothing, *no one*, can ever take my love for him away.

That's why we are to be bound as soon as he can make the arrangements."

Raphael's face lit up. "This is wonderful news!"

"You're happy about it?" Lash asked.

"Of course. I am not the same person Lucifer showed you in your memories. It may have taken losing you and Jeremiel to realize how wrong I was back then. Can you forgive me for my past, for my inability to be a good father to you?"

Lash looked at Raphael's pleading eyes. In all the time he'd known him, at least the times he could remember, Raphael had always been by his side, guiding him, helping him. Even when he did his best to push Raphael away, he never left. And now he knew why. Raphael was trying his best to make it up to him, to be a better father. "Yes...Father."

Raphael's face lit up. "You make me proud—both of you."

He stood and pulled Lash into his arms. Surprised, Lash looked over to Naomi. Tears glistened in her eyes as she watched them.

"Hug him back," she mouthed.

He nodded and placed a hand on Raphael's back, giving him a gentle squeeze. He felt warmth spread through him, a peace he hadn't felt for a long time.

"I shall go with you to visit Michael," Raphael said when he pulled back. "At long last, I have my family back with me. This is a joyous occasion. Is it not, Jeremiel?"

Jeremy stood and approached Lash, extending his hand to him. "Congratulations. I wish you both everlasting happiness."

Lash looked down at his hand and then back at his face. The only thing he saw was the sincerity in his eyes. He really was happy for him.

He took Jeremy's hand, and for a moment, he felt that maybe, just maybe, he had his old friend back.

And then he watched as Jeremy turned to Naomi. He was barely able to look at her as he mumbled his congratulations and called her sister.

# 5

"Are you sure about this?" Naomi scanned the area surrounding the stream to make sure no one was around to see her and Lash stepping onto the bridge. Her heart fluttered with excitement at the thought of seeing Welita and Chuy again, although she wished Lash would let her do this alone. If she were caught disobeying Gabrielle's orders, they might let it slide for her since she was new. But if Lash were caught, he might get in trouble for helping her.

"Absolutely." He took hold of her hand as they went to the center of the bridge. "I'll keep a look out for you."

Naomi bit down on her lip. She was only seconds away from seeing Welita after all these weeks. Why was she suddenly afraid to look?

"What's wrong?"

She gazed into his beautiful hazel eyes. How could she ever be afraid with him by her side? She was being silly. "Nothing. I'll make this real quick."

She went to the spot where she knew she could get the best view of Welita's house. Her hand brushed over the familiar railing. Again, her heart raced in anticipation.

*Knock it off,* she told herself. *Stop making a big deal about this. You've looked in on Welita lots of times.*

Taking a deep breath, she leaned over the rail. The water was still. It was like looking through smooth glass. For a moment, she saw nothing but the clear water. Then slowly, the familiar small white house emerged.

Her heart slammed against her chest. Something was wrong. Something was off.

The once lush green and perfectly manicured lawn was filled with knee-high weeds. The flowerbeds that Welita so meticulously cared for, her pride and joy, were overrun with crab grass and littered with beer cans.

She slammed her eyes shut. This couldn't be Welita's house. She took a deep breath, trying to calm herself. *Don't panic.*

She was obviously looking in the wrong direction. She just had to be more careful.

When she slowly opened her eyes, she saw the same small white house in the same place. She moaned.

*It is Welita's house.*

Shattered glass littered the front porch, and the screen door banged loosely in the wind. Worst of all, every single window was broken.

What happened? Welita and Chuy would never let the house look like that, unless...the house was empty.

"No!" She wailed as she threw herself against the rail, leaning over as far as she could. The house was Welita's pride and joy. She would never leave it. Her father grew up in that house. Something had to have happened—something so awful that Welita had no choice but to leave.

Fear stuck in her throat as she thought of the one thing that could pull her stubborn grandmother away from her home.

No! No way! Welita was not dead. There was no way that could happen. Welita had been in the best of health when she last saw her a few weeks ago. It had to be something else. It just had to be.

Frantic, she ran along the side of the bridge, trying to get a better look at the surrounding neighborhood, desperate to find a clue, anything to explain what had happened to Welita and Chuy.

"What's wrong?" Lash followed close behind her.

"Welita's gone." She sobbed.

She looked at the other houses near Welita's. They all had the same haunted, broken-down appearance. It looked like the entire neighborhood had been abandoned. "They're all gone!"

"What? Are you sure?" He leaned over the railing and peered at the water.

"I-I don't understand. It's only been a few weeks since I last saw her. Everything looked normal. There were cars lining the street. The neighborhood kids were playing basketball. Everything looked exactly like it did when I left."

"It's been a few weeks," he mumbled.

"Yeah, an entire neighborhood block can't just up and leave in a couple of weeks, can it? I mean look at the grass. It's almost knee deep!"

He pinched the bridge of his nose and gritted his teeth. "A few weeks," he repeated.

"Why do you keep saying that?"

He groaned and then slammed his hand against the railing. "Shit!"

"What? What is it?"

He paced the length of the bridge, running his hands through his hair and cursing under his breath.

"I didn't think anything like this would happen," he mumbled as he dropped his head into his hands. "Stupid, stupid, stupid!"

"Lash, please tell me. You know something." Her voice grew louder with each word. She grabbed his shoulders when he wouldn't answer, shaking him. "Tell me!"

Tormented eyes met hers. "It was a few weeks...for you."

She blinked, confused. "For me? What do you mean, for me?"

"Well, for us actually." He turned his head away, unable to look at her. "I can't believe I didn't tell you."

She placed a hand under his chin and directed it towards her. "Tell me what?"

He inhaled sharply and held his breath before he let it out in a rush. "Time is different here than it is on Earth."

"What does that mean? Time is different? How different?"

Her heart dropped to the pit of her stomach. *Oh, God! Maybe they're all dead.*

Lash's face zoomed in and out of focus, and she felt herself falling.

"Naomi!" He cried as he caught her.

"How...long?" Her voice was soft, fearful.

"You're in shock. Let's get you back home. I'm so sorry I forgot to tell you. I can explain it all to you and then we can figure out—"

"No." She took a deep breath and forced herself to stand. Now was not the time to be weak. Now was time to be the archangel she was training to become. Taking another fortifying breath, she said, "Tell me. How long has it been?"

"I never really paid much attention to time. We don't measure time here like on Earth. I'd say maybe"—he gulped and eyed her with worry—"a year."

"A year! I've been gone for a year?"

"Maybe less," he said frantically.

She let out a breath. She should be thankful that it was only a year. She turned and stared down at Welita's house. She had planned to sneak in a visit when she was given her first assignment. She had wanted to give Welita some kind of sign that she was still with her. Even if Welita wasn't able to see her, she knew Welita would know it was her.

She'd even planned on seeing Chuy, knowing that he too had grown to believe that angels did exist. Now, they were gone.

A sudden thought hit her. "Archangels are powerful. They can pretty much do anything, right?"

"I wouldn't say anything, but, yeah, they have powerful gifts. Why?"

"I can find them."

"You won't be able to go down to Earth unless you are given an assignment or one of the archangels gives you permission."

"But *I'm* an archangel."

"Technically, yeah, you're an archangel, but you're in training. You'll still need approval from Michael or Gabrielle, and they would never give it, unless it was to serve some higher purpose."

Her face dropped. What was the use of being an archangel with power if you couldn't use it? What was she going to do now? Tears slid down her face. "I thought Heaven was supposed to be a happy place."

He gathered her into his arms. "Naomi, please don't cry."

She couldn't help it. She wanted to be brave, to be the powerful archangel they expected her to be. She couldn't. It was hard, so hard to leave a part of herself, the part that made her who she was, behind, her family: Welita, Chuy, her parents. Having them made her feel like she could do anything. When her parents died, she'd felt like she lost a little bit of that. And now, with Welita and Chuy gone, it felt like she was left with a hole in her chest.

Lash placed a finger under her chin and lifted it up to meet his eyes. "I'll take you to find Welita."

"How?" She sniffed. "You don't know where they are."

"I have a plan. Go back home, and when I return, I'll have the permission you and I need to go down to Earth."

Her eyes widened. "I don't want you to do anything to get kicked out. I can't lose you too." She wanted to find her family desperately, but not at his expense.

"It's perfectly legit. I promise. I can't tell you now. Just know that I'll get it for you. Do you trust me?"

She looked into his glorious face, and his eyes gazed at her tenderly. She sighed, feeling hopeful. With Lash by her side, they could do anything.

"Yes."

Lash trudged down a worn path alongside the stream, a path he had taken hundreds of times over the years. *I can't believe I'm actually doing this.*

He had promised Naomi that he'd get her to Earth to find Welita and Chuy. Thinking they would surely empathize with Naomi's situation, his first thought was to ask Rachel or Uri for permission. He axed that idea when he remembered all they had gone through and the centuries of separation from each other. It wouldn't be fair to ask them, only for them to get in trouble. Archangels were not safe from being punished. Raphael could attest to that.

That only left one person who could help him, and it irritated him to no end that Lash had to ask him for help.

He shuffled slowly up the flower-lined path to Jeremy's door. Jeremy lived in a one-room cottage along the stream, a few miles away from the bridge that was a gateway to Earth. Like his clothes, Jeremy kept his living quarters spotless, which was a difficult thing to do, especially after poker night. Even when Lash had offered to host, Jeremy refused, claiming no one would be able to get through the front door with the mountain of mess in his room.

Jeremy did his job like he led his life. Everything had its place and purpose. Although lately, he didn't seem to be his usual self.

Lash tried to shake the memory of the way Jeremy acted around Naomi last night. Deep down, he knew Jeremy was truly happy for him and his announcement that he would be bound to Naomi soon. Then why did he feel like he couldn't trust Jeremy near her?

It didn't help that he had to ask Jeremy for a favor. He hadn't minded before, but now, things were different.

He knew Jeremy was eager to prove himself as a true friend and brother to him, and he was confident Jeremy would say yes. And that was the problem. *He* wanted to be the one to give Naomi what she needed to make her happy. Not Jeremy.

He was about to knock on the cottage door when he heard a whistling in the distance, followed by a loud splash of water. That could only mean one thing—Jeremy was swimming.

When he approached the stream, he paused and leaned against a tree, watching Jeremy swim. He remembered what Raphael had told him about Jeremy being favored by others. Now he saw him with new eyes.

Jeremy's body was tanned golden by the rays of the sun, whereas Lash was pale in comparison. Jeremy's thick arms moved effortlessly through the water, and Lash gritted his teeth as he noted the size of them. Where Lash was tall and lithe, Jeremy was huge and muscular. All the years he'd known Jeremy, he had never noticed or even cared. So, why now?

"Lash!" Jeremy cried when he saw him. "What brings you here?"

Lash's stomach twisted with envy as he watched Jeremy step out of the stream and head towards him, perfect white teeth flashing him a smile. He was taller, stronger, and loved by all the other angels. Lash could never compete with him, and for a brief moment, he wondered what Naomi had ever seen in him. Were her feelings for Jeremy buried along with her memories? What if she got them back?

*Knock it off! Naomi is not like that. She loves me.* He felt her love every time she looked at him. That would never change.

And Jeremy? He had to believe Jeremy would never do anything to hurt him or Naomi.

He focused his thoughts on Naomi. Her needs came first. Swallowing his pride and forcing a smile on his face, he said, "I need a favor."

# 6

There was a light crunching sound when Lash's feet landed on the dead grass covering Welita's backyard. The house looked worse than when they saw it from Heaven. It was as if the life that once filled the home, the entire neighborhood, had been sucked out and all that was left was a skeleton.

He reached out to grab Naomi's hand, knowing she would be heartbroken.

He watched Naomi bite down on her lip, her pale blue eyes watering. "Are you okay?"

"Yeah, just give me a moment." Her voice quivered.

"Don't you want to go inside? Maybe we can find some clues as to where they are."

She nodded. Her face was a mixture of emotions. "Yes, I do. It's just, everything is so different. I mean, it's more than just the empty house. It feels different. I don't know why. I feel like I've lost something, or someone."

"Maybe it's because you're different."

"How? It hasn't been long...well, at least for me it doesn't feel like it's been that long."

He gathered her into his arms and kissed her forehead. "So much has happened to you in such a short amount of time. It's not surprising that you'd be confused. Part of you still feels like it belongs in this world."

"I don't know who I'm supposed to be: Welita's granddaughter or Heaven's seventh archangel."

"You're young for an angel, and it's so rare for humans to be placed with us." He gave her a gentle squeeze. "I'll help you through this. I promise."

"I know you will."

"Why don't we look around the outside and then work our way in, okay?"

They walked hand in hand toward the front, passing through the weeds and overgrown rosebushes. Naomi bent down to touch the wilting flowers, stifling a sob. "Welita's roses. Chuy and I worked with her for days planting them around the house. She talked to them, you know."

"Really?"

"Yeah. She watered and talked to them all the time. They were gorgeous. And their fragrance..." She let out a breath. "You could smell them from down the street. They smelled so good. And now, she's gone, and they're gone."

Her fingers glided over the browning stems. "She said flowers had feelings too. I think she was right."

He squeezed her hand, trying to comfort her. As they continued walking through the tall grass, his foot hit a small plastic object. He bent down and smiled sadly as he picked up a dog dish.

He stared at the red dish, surprised when his eyes pricked with the threat of tears. He recalled how he'd hide behind the bushes and Bear would dash to him like a little furry jet. Ignoring the dog food in the bowl, she'd run around his feet until he gave her the little sausages he'd bought just for her. He'd grumble at her as he took the smelly dish and disposed the contents with not even a lick of thank you.

*Ungrateful dog,* he thought as a lump formed in his throat.

He swallowed thickly. "Let's see what we can find in the front."

The front yard didn't look any different from the back. Trash littered the steps of the house. Beer cans, bottles, an old sock. Graffiti was written on the front walls.

"Don't do that," he said when Naomi bent down and picked up a flattened basketball.

"Why? I want to clean up."

"You're in your angel form. No one can see you. If someone passes by, they'll only see the objects in your hand and not you."

"Oh, right." She dropped the deflated ball. "I forgot about that. Can we change into human form?"

He looked around the neighborhood. It didn't seem like anyone was nearby. But if one of her old neighbors just happened to be around or if they ran into someone who knew her, it could be trouble for them, especially since they thought she was dead. "I don't want to take a chance on someone seeing you."

"Okay." She glanced over his shoulder and furrowed her brow. "Is that a sign over there? I don't remember seeing it before."

They headed toward a large sign on the corner of the street. Lash scanned the area as they walked over, studying each of the houses as they passed. Other than a few stray cats that scrambled underneath a house porch when they passed, it was obvious no one had lived in any of the homes for quite some time. He listened carefully for any sounds of life in the surrounding area. There was nothing.

The entire neighborhood for blocks around was empty.

His hand dropped from Naomi's grasp as she placed it over her mouth. His heart slammed into full gear when her face grew shockingly white.

"What is it?"

She shook her head, and tears streamed down her face as she pointed to the sign.

A numbing cold washed over him as he read it.

*Future site of Prescott Park.*

*Houston luxury living at its finest.*

Lash held Naomi as they sat on the porch steps of Welita's abandoned home. He should have known that Lucifer, known to people on Earth as the billionaire Luke Prescott, was behind this. How could he have been so stupid to think he'd stop? Naomi was in Heaven. She was an archangel now or at least in training. Lucifer was up to something—he just didn't know what.

"It's my fault. I did this to Welita, to Chuy, to the entire neighborhood!" Naomi bawled, dropping her head into her hands.

"It's not your fault." His voice was gentle as he stroked her back. "The battle between the angels and Lucifer has been going on for centuries."

"Yes, but he's after *me*. He wants me dead because I'm the seventh archangel." She popped up her head and looked at him with a glint in her eyes. "I can fix this. Maybe if I go to him and work out a deal—"

"No! Absolutely not."

"But, I—"

He pressed a finger to her lips, silencing her, and she scowled.

Kissing her lightly, he said, "It wouldn't make any difference if you did. Think about it. The purpose of killing you when you were human was to prevent you from becoming an archangel, which you will be, once your training is complete."

"Then why is he after my family?"

"I don't know. We need to talk to Raphael. Maybe he'll know what Lucifer is up to."

"Oh, my God!" She gripped his arm, her eyes bulging with terror. "What if he killed them? What if he killed them all?"

"He wouldn't do that. That would be a lot of people to kill, and it would get way too much media attention," he said calmly. "He has to maintain his position here on Earth."

"He wouldn't have to do it himself. He could've gotten Sal to do it or his other followers."

He shook his head. "It doesn't make sense why he would."

A muffled sound came from inside the house.

He stiffened. "What was that?"

Naomi stood and headed toward to door.

"Wait!" He jumped, grabbing her arm. "It could be one of them."

"Let go." She tugged at her arm. "They might know where Welita and Chuy are."

He tightened his grip. There was no way he was letting her go in there. If there were more than one of them, he didn't know if they could fight them off. "Even if they do know, they won't tell you."

"Lash," she warned, her eyes blazing with determination. "I'm going in."

He let out a breath. There was no stopping her when she had her mind made up. He loved that about her—except when it placed her in the line of possible danger.

"Okay, but let me go in first. Stay behind me, and if anything happens, leave. Go to Raphael and let him know."

She hesitated a moment before finally giving in with a grumble and moving aside to let him pass.

"Stubborn woman," he said as he kissed her forehead.

As he went in, he heard the muffled sounds coming from the hall to the right of him.

"I think it's coming from Welita's room," Naomi whispered.

He nodded and moved slowly down the hall. Just as he reached the entrance to the bedroom, a woman's silhouette appeared in the doorway.

He moved back and placed his arm up, holding Naomi away from the stranger.

The silhouette moved slowly toward them. Lash was about to attack when the shadow stepped into the sunlit hall, and hazel eyes locked with his.

"Lahash."

Lash froze with shock at the petite angel who gazed lovingly at him. Dark waves of hair cascaded onto her shoulders. She wore a pink dress that flowed down to her ankles. The delicate dress, with tiny billowy sleeves and lace trim, flowed around her with each step she took.

Something inside of him stirred as he watched her. Something he hadn't felt since the first time he heard that same voice calling out his name. It was a feeling of unconditional love. He saw it in her eyes. The only other person who looked at him like that, other than Naomi, was Raphael.

"Rebecca?" Naomi stepped around Lash. "Are you Rebecca?"

A tender smile lit her face. "Yes, how did you know?"

"You look just like Lash—so beautiful." Naomi nudged him. "Are you all right? You're so quiet."

"I-I-I..." He gulped, overwhelmed with emotion. "I don't know what to say."

It felt like only yesterday he had found out about his parents. When Raphael told him that his punishment was to never see her again, Lash had thought he'd never have a chance to meet her. And now, here she was, standing in Welita's house.

"It's been a long time, Lahash," Rebecca said. "Has Raphael explained to you who I am?"

"Yes. You're"—he took a deep breath—"you're my mother."

"I am." She stopped a few inches from him, and her eyes took him in with wonder.

"May I?"

He tensed as she wrapped her arms around him and placed her head on his chest. His shirt grew moist from the tears that fell. Slowly, he relaxed and placed his hands around her. She was so small, delicate. His hands touched her velvety hair, and a memory stirred deep within him, fighting to get out.

He squeezed his eyes shut, wanting desperately to have his memories of her resurface. All he could see were bits and pieces, images of her holding him, playing with him as a small child.

And then a feeling slowly spread through his body, a feeling like none he'd ever had before. It was as if there had been an empty place in his chest, a place he didn't even know was missing, and it was slowly being filled up with motherly love.

He held her tighter.

Cradling him in her arms, she crooned, "Lahash, my son. I have missed you so."

"Mother," he croaked. His memories of her may have been suppressed, but this, the warmth, the love he felt was there with him.

She pulled back, tears staining her cheeks. "I don't have much time with you, and there is much I need to tell you."

"Wait." There was something he had to do before anything else. Something he'd always wanted to do but didn't think he'd ever have the chance.

He turned and took Naomi's hand, pulling her next to him. "This is my Naomi—the love of my life. We are to be bound."

Hazel eyes lit up, and she placed a hand over her heart. "Oh, Lahash, you don't know what great joy it brings me to have you two together again, after all these centuries. When I found out you were assigned to her, I knew—well, I hoped—that you two would find love again."

Rebecca turned to Naomi and, reaching over with her small hand, cupped her cheek. "You do your grandmother proud, Naomi. She is the reason why I am here."

"Where is she? Is she all right?"

"She's doing well now, and she's with your cousin, Chuy."

"Now? What do you mean, now?"

Rebecca took her hand, and her face grew serious. "Don't be alarmed when I tell you this. She had a heart attack soon after you left."

"She had a heart attack?" Naomi's voice grew frantic. "We need to find her. I need to go to her now. Please tell me where she is."

"Your grandmother is not in any immediate danger," Rebecca said calmly. "Chuy saw to her every need, and she was given the best medical care. She was given a pacemaker, and it helps her tremendously, but..." She looked at Naomi with worry. "They struggled with the finances."

"Oh, Chuy," Naomi sobbed. "I should've been here."

Rebecca shook her head. "It was the first time I heard him pray."

"Chuy prayed?"

She nodded. "It broke my heart. In all the time I've watched over your grandmother, it was the only time he'd asked for help, other than the time when you were in the hospital."

Lash wrapped a hand around Naomi's shoulder. He felt so helpless watching the guilt eat her up from the inside. He had to find Welita and Chuy for her. "Where are they? Why did they leave?"

Rebecca sighed. "They held out as long as they could. Chuy took on a second job to pay off the bills, even his friend tried to help him out."

"Who? Lalo?" Naomi asked.

"Yes, Lalo. What a fine young man. He was devastated when his father decided to sell off his moving business."

"Mr. Cruz sold his business!" Naomi cried in disbelief.

"He wanted to retire, and when representatives from Prescott Oil came into the neighborhood, they bought up the surrounding local businesses first. Mr. Cruz was the first to take their offer. But it wasn't too long before the others followed."

"No." Naomi paled.

"I'm afraid so. Then after that, they made offers to the property owners, for the homes in the neighborhood. As you know, many of your neighbors rented their homes and had no choice."

"But Welita owned her house."

"She was the last to hold out. But with the mounting medical bills and Chuy needing a job, they had to move. So, Welita finally agreed." Rebecca placed a hand on her shoulder. "It wasn't easy for them. Welita wanted to stay."

Naomi sank to the floor. She tucked her knees up to her chest and dropped her head. "I knew it was my fault. They drove them out because of me."

Rebecca glanced at Lash with a sad, knowing look on her face before sitting down next to Naomi.

"Naomi, none of this is your doing. They're safe. They live in North Texas now. Chuy placed her in an assisted-living facility so there would be someone looking after her while he and Lalo work. They live just outside of Gardenville."

*We're new to the city. Just moved here from Gardenville.* Lash recalled Nathan's teasing voice when he teased his wife, Deborah, about having to be careful living in a big city like Houston.

He felt the hair on the back of his neck stand up. It seemed like Welita and Chuy had been intentionally directed to North Texas. But why?

"I don't get it," he said. "Why go all the way to North Texas to work? Why not get a job here in Houston?"

"He was offered a very well-paying job there."

"Where?" He asked.

She glanced at Naomi and then back at him. "Prescott Oil."

"Prescott Oil? Prescott Oil!" Naomi slammed her hand against the floor. "You mean the same Prescott Oil that bought them out? The same Prescott Oil owned by Lucifer?"

"Yes."

"Oh, Chuy," she moaned and banged the back of her head on the wall. "If he knew who Luke Prescott was, he'd have never taken the job. Wait!" Naomi jumped up, her face looking hopeful. "You can tell them. You're Welita's guardian angel. Can't you do that? Can't you warn them?"

"It doesn't work that way, Naomi." Her voice was gentle. "We're not allowed to interfere with human will."

"But we're not interfering. We're just providing them with information." Naomi's face scrunched in frustration.

"Please believe me." She stood and went to Naomi. "If it were in my power to do so, I would tell them. And I'm not her guardian angel anymore. My work with her is done. I'm only here because I knew you would worry, and I wanted to let you know what happened."

"What? So who's looking after her? And what about Chuy?" Naomi paced the length of the hall. "It's not right. We can't just leave them like this. We can't let Lucifer use them as pawns in whatever crazy scheme he's up to. Tell her, Lash."

Lash gaped at her, wishing he could support her. He wanted to so badly. How could he explain to her the ramifications if they helped or that she'd lost her father because of his interference thirty-five years ago?

"Naomi, I've made the mistake before. It'll put too much at risk if we interfere. Believe me, I know."

Her face filled with pain. "I thought you were on my side."

"I *am* on your side. It's just..." He felt like kicking himself. She didn't know he was the one who'd saved Jane, who'd been meant to die on that plane so many years ago. The same Jane who had killed her father.

"What?"

"I..." He glanced over at Rebecca, and she gazed back at him knowingly. Instead of being bothered that she knew, he felt comforted. But how did she know? She was forbidden to see Raphael, so he hadn't told her, but somehow, she knew. "I don't want you to make the same mistakes I did."

Naomi reached out to him and placed her hand on his chest. "It can't be a mistake to care for the ones you love."

"Naomi, you're new to our world. There are rules in place for all of our protection," Rebecca said.

"Sometimes, rules need to be broken." She turned back to Lash. "You broke them to be with me."

"And I'd do it again, just to be with you."

"So why not break this rule, for me?" she breathed, begging him.

"You need to tell her, Lahash," Rebecca said softly. "No more secrets."

"Tell me what?" Naomi asked.

Lash glanced at Rebecca, and she nodded with encouragement. This secret was a burden he'd carried with him ever since he fell in love with Naomi, and fear of what she'd do if she knew nagged at the back of his mind constantly. His mother was right. He had to tell Naomi his secret about her father's death. If they were to be bound together, he had to be truthful with her.

He picked up her hands and kissed them. Then, he squeezed his eyes shut and prayed for the strength.

"Lash?" Her voice sounded worried.

He opened his eyes and looked deeply into hers. "No matter what happens, know that I love you more than my own life."

"You're scaring me."

He took a deep breath. "I was waiting for the right time to tell you this. And, well, there is just no right time. I never told you about the assignment that got me kicked out of Heaven."

"No, you didn't."

"I was sent to watch over a little boy. A boy named Javier Duran."

She inhaled sharply. "It *was* you. You saved him from the plane explosion. Welita told me it could only have been from divine intervention that he was saved. I thought it was luck because of where he was sitting. He was behind a twelve-year-old girl, right?"

He nodded. "Welita didn't tell you who the little girl was?

"No. I didn't think it was important to ask." She furrowed her brow. "Why?"

"Well, the girl made it out alive because I saved her and she"—he gulped—"she wasn't meant to live."

"Why not? She was just a little girl."

"Because she ended up being with Lucifer, and..." He looked over to Rebecca, who smiled sadly, her eyes shone with love and support. "That little girl was Jane Sutherland."

There was a beat of silence.

Naomi's face grew pale as she stepped away from him. "No," her voice was barely above a whisper. "That's not true. Tell me that's not true."

"Naomi." He reached out to her, his heart breaking into pieces. "I'm sorry."

She jerked back and shook her head, tears streaming down her face. "Don't touch me."

"Please, Naomi."

"No, I can't. I just...can't." She spun and fled out of the house.

"Naomi!"

He tore out of the house chasing after her. She shot high into the sky, her wings spread at full length, giving her the power to out-fly him.

He pushed with all his might to try to catch her. If he could only reach her, he could explain everything. Then maybe, just maybe she would understand and forgive him.

Faster, he soared up higher and higher. With one final push, he got close enough to reach out and grab her shoulders. He turned her to face him, and his heart stopped at the shattered look on her face.

"Naomi, I—"

"Don't." Her voice was raw. "I can't be with you right now."

He inhaled sharply as the pain in his chest crushed him. She looked at him one last time, turned, and flew away.

# 7

Not knowing where else to go, Naomi paced the path that went through the cherry tree gardens. It hurt too much to go to the mountain home she and Lash shared. Being in the beautiful gardens didn't help, either. Everywhere she looked, she thought of Lash: his beautiful hazel eyes, his strong arms around her, the feel of his unshaven jaw against her palm, and then the torment in his eyes when he told her about saving Jane Sutherland.

She felt her heart breaking as she struggled between her love for her father and her love for Lash. If only he had listened to his orders, then she would still have her father.

She remembered the last time she saw him. It had been at her college graduation. She recalled the proud look he wore as she walked toward him with her diploma in hand.

She smiled as she thought of him sitting on the porch next to her as they both gazed up at the stars that night.

She sank onto a bench under one of the dozens of cherry trees. A breeze blew gently, causing stands of her dark hair to brush against her face.

She was so confused. If she accepted that her father dying was somehow Lash's fault, then how could she continue to love the person who basically shortened her father's life? But then, if that hadn't happened, she would've never known the love of her life.

She tilted her head back to look at the clear blue sky.

Why was this all happening to her? Fate. Free-will. Had Lash put something into motion that wasn't meant to be? Was she meant to have lived her life on Earth with her father, her family?

She burst into tears. She couldn't give Lash up, but she couldn't even bear to look at him. She felt so lost. For weeks, she had struggled with missing her family. She wanted more than anything to feel like she belonged in Heaven, to have a home with Lash. And now, now it felt like Heaven was her Hell.

She heard footsteps approaching and quickly wiped the tears from her eyes.

"Raphael," she croaked. She cleared her throat and forced a smile on her face. "How are you this morning?"

Raphael looked into her eyes, reached out, and brushed a stray tear from her cheek. "He told you."

She nodded, choking back fresh tears.

"It is not easy being an angel, and to be an archangel, that can be even more difficult. Lahash has great compassion for others. It leads him to be ruled by his heart rather than by what his superiors tell him to do."

"It's not supposed to be like this. My father should still be alive. I'm supposed to be with him and Welita."

"Perhaps," he said. "Or maybe things are exactly the way they should be."

She looked at him, surprised. "Are you saying his disobedience was meant to be?"

"I was just as surprised as Lahash when he was thrown out. For years, I went to Michael, advocating his return. Now, I am not quite sure of this, but it seems to me there is something larger at work here."

More secrets. She couldn't take it anymore. "This is too much. I can't think right now."

Raphael looked over her shoulder and spoke softly. "Gabrielle and Jeremiel are coming. I can divert them if you wish."

She let out a breath. "No, I'll be fine."

She needed a distraction, anything to get her mind off how miserable she was feeling at that moment. Burying herself in training with Gabrielle was just what she needed right now.

Squaring her shoulders, she stood to greet her. "Gabrielle, I'm sorry for the late start, but I'm ready for my training session now. Is Jeremy joining us today?"

Seeing Gabrielle's green eyes dart from Raphael to her, Naomi hoped her eyes weren't too red and puffy, although she knew her voice sounded strained. She must've looked awful because Jeremy kept staring at her strangely.

"There's other business we must attend to today. Where's Lash?"

"Uh, he's—"

"He's in the Room of Offerings, repairing some of the damage," Raphael interrupted.

Naomi shot him a surprised look. Raphael could be sneaky when he wanted to be. Lash had told her about the mess he'd made when he thought he'd never see her again. She had wanted to go with him to help him clean it up, but he'd kept putting it off.

"I see," Gabrielle said, looking suspiciously at him. "It's taken him long enough to do so. Well, then, let's get straight to the business at hand, shall we?"

Gabrielle handed her a small white envelope. As she took a hold of it, Gabrielle looked intently into her eyes. "It is of utmost importance that you stick to your assignment at all costs. Do you understand?"

"Yes, I do," she said quickly.

Gabrielle continued to hold on to the envelope. "Although you are moving along quite nicely in your training, I fear you are not fully invested in the role you've been given. However, events have taken place that make this assignment necessary."

Naomi dropped her hand at the seriousness of Gabrielle's voice. She wasn't ready to take on something like this. "Maybe it's better to send someone else."

"Michael made specific instructions for you to carry this assignment, and Jeremy is to go with you."

"I hope you don't mind the company," he said, his dimples flashing as he smiled at her.

"N-n-no. It's just...uh, well, after last night, I'm not sure if that's such a good idea." As angry and hurt as she was with Lash right now, she didn't want to make things any worse. Although Lash appeared to have made peace with Jeremy, even asking him to give them permission to go down to Earth, she couldn't shake the feeling that Lash still had a problem with him.

"You have no choice in this matter," Gabrielle snapped. "Jeremy is to accompany you. He'll serve as a mentor to you as well as taking care of his own assignment."

Naomi glanced at him. With Jeremy going with her, maybe she could search for Welita. If it were Gabrielle, she'd never be allowed to do it.

"Okay," she said as she reached for the envelope and pulled out the card containing information about her assignment. "When do we—holy shit! This isn't...this can't be..."

She slapped a hand across her mouth, mortified.

Gabrielle's face turned a bright red. "We do not use such foul language here."

"Aw, come on, Gabrielle," Jeremy said. "Don't tell me you haven't thrown around a cuss word or two when Lash was around."

She narrowed her eyes at him. "Never."

"Cut the girl some slack. She's just in a bit of shock."

"It is her first assignment, Gabrielle." Raphael added, placing a hand on her shoulder.

Her face softened. "Fine, just mind your tongue, Naomi."

"I'm sorry," Naomi said. "This just isn't someone I expected to ever have to watch over. So, when do we leave?"

"We'll need to head out right away," Jeremy replied. "We can stop by the Room of Offerings so you can say bye to Lash before we head out."

"Why would you say bye to me?"

Naomi spun around at the sound of Lash's voice. His face was a mask. The pain in her chest resurfaced, and she found it hard to breathe. She turned away, unable to look at him.

"Michael has given Naomi an assignment," Raphael said. "Jeremy is to accompany her. They're leaving at once."

Naomi could feel Lash's eyes on her. She wanted to look at him. She wanted to forget everything he had told her. She wanted her Lash back. But, she couldn't take those words away.

"I see." Lash's voice was cold.

Taking a deep breath, she looked to Jeremy. "I'm ready."

"Don't you"—Jeremy's eyes bounced between her and Lash, puzzled—"uh, okay then, come with me."

She stared down at his hand as he held it out to her. Her head turned slightly, fighting the desire to see Lash one last time before she left. She couldn't look at him, not now, especially if she wanted to focus on the assignment she'd been given. Slowly, she placed her hand into Jeremy's, and then they were gone.

It took every ounce of strength for Lash not to cry out to Naomi as he watched her place her hand into Jeremy's. He kept repeating to himself that she'd been given an assignment, that Jeremy was just doing his job as an archangel. But with what Raphael had said about Jeremy wanting Naomi so long ago, and the way he'd looked at her last night, he couldn't forget it.

"Lash, I would like to speak to you in private," Raphael said. "Gabrielle, if you don't mind."

"Of course. I'll be with Michael," she said and then disappeared.

Lash slumped on the bench. "Did you know about this?"

"I was told about it some time ago. I didn't think it would happen this soon. Something must have changed to speed up the events."

"You knew Jeremy was to go with her? Why didn't you tell me?"

Raphael gave him a stern look.

"Right. You archangel, me lowly seraph. You'd think I would've learned that by now."

Raphael let out a breath as he sat next to him. "You told her about saving the girl."

"She didn't take it very well, and now she's gone." Lash leaned forward, placing his forearms on his knees. "She couldn't even look at me."

He dropped his head against his chest, not wanting Raphael to see the tears forming in his eyes. The look of pain and betrayal on her face was seared into his mind. She didn't have to say goodbye to him—her silence said it for her.

"My son, she is not gone forever. She's merely off on assignment. She will return to you."

"I know she'll come back, but will she come back to *me*? Can she forgive me?"

"Naomi loves you, and I have faith in her."

Lash shook his head. He wanted to believe in her love. He wanted to so badly. He just couldn't shake off that look.

He felt Raphael's hand pat his back. "Think of it this way: she'll have time to think this through, and I know she will understand that you meant no harm."

"I don't know if I can do it, wait so long without going crazy." Even though time went faster in Heaven than Earth, each second seemed like hours to him.

"How did you do it, Raphael? How do you make it through all that time without seeing Rebecca? The thought of being away from Naomi for even a day leaves me breathless."

Raphael swallowed thickly. "It is…difficult."

Lash looked up at Raphael and wondered if he should tell him about seeing Rebecca. Would it hurt him more if he did?

*Crap! I can't tell him.* Only Jeremy knew about them going down to Earth.

"Son, you'll be with her again soon," he continued. "Mark my words. And once you are, she will need you to be there for her. Just as you were tested, she too will be tested in her faith and loyalty to her Heavenly family."

"Naomi is strong."

"That may be, but I fear that Naomi and Jeremy's assignment will test her limits. And she has been here for such a short time."

"She gets along with everybody. I don't think she'll have a hard time with it. Who's her assignment?"

"You and I know her well. You may know her just a bit more so than I."

Lash's brow furrowed. "What do you mean?"

"You have carnal knowledge of this person."

"Who?" he squeaked.

"Megan. Megan Dalene."

# 8

Jane Sutherland tapped a pen against the desk as she read her tenth newspaper that morning. She scribbled on her yellow note pad furiously as she read the opinion page. Each paper she went through bashed her position on environmental policies. Most of them even dared to claim that she didn't care for families or the community and instead sided with big business. Being a senator, she'd thought she would get used to being questioned about her voting record. She even accepted the fact that she'd be scrutinized because she was a close friend with Luke Prescott. Regardless, it still stung to read what people thought of her and her closest confidant.

If only people could know the Luke she'd known almost all her life—kind, protective, sometimes overly protective.

But saying she didn't care about the people in her own home state of Texas—that was going too far.

"Jane, dear, how many times have I told you reading the papers will make you old before your time?"

She looked up from the paper to see a pair of kind gray eyes gazing at her.

"I know; I know." She sighed. "I'm just working on my speech."

"We have speech writers on staff for that. Use them." Luke sat on the sofa across from her desk and placed a cup and saucer on the coffee table. "They're the best in the field."

"I'm sure they are. Announcing that I'm running for the presidency is very important to me. I want to get it right."

"Even more reason to use a speech writer."

"This is personal for me, Luke. I'm doing this because I truly believe I can make a difference. The American Federation party can make our country better for everyone."

"Spoken like a true politician." He grinned.

She rolled her eyes. "I mean it, Luke."

"Then use what we have at our disposal. This is going to be a long campaign, and we're fortunate to have plenty of financial resources."

"That's the problem." She sighed as she picked up a newspaper from the stack in the middle of her desk and waved it at him. "How can I touch the hearts of the people in this country when the media portray me to be out of touch with Middle America? I have to figure out a way to make them see that what our party is doing is good for all."

He tugged on the sleeves of his crisp white shirt. Small diamond cufflinks twinkled as the light hit them. "What are they complaining about now?"

"Fracking." Jane searched through the pile of newspapers, pulled one out, and tossed it to him. "This one says that the fracking Prescott Oil is doing in North Texas is causing the earthquakes in the area."

Luke laughed. "I was told on good authority that the seismic events barely registered. Besides, we have our own geophysicists, *Harvard*-based, mind you, who say it is a natural shift in the plates in that area."

She pursed her lips before continuing. "Then there is this paper." She waved it. "They have a reporter doing an undercover investigation in Gardenville."

She got up from her desk, sat in the seat across from Luke, and handed the paper to him. "He claims the wells aren't safe and that chemicals used in the fracking process are seeping into the drinking water."

"Absurd! There is absolutely no proof." Luke tossed the paper onto the table. "Besides, Texas has some of the most stringent regulations in the country."

"That may be, but I've received word that State Representative James Keith will be introducing a bill requiring companies to disclose the chemical used in the fracking fluid."

Jane felt an eerie chill at the blank expression on Luke's face. It wasn't a look she'd ever seen on him before.

His lips slowly curled into a smile that didn't reach his eyes, and she shivered. "It sounds like an environmental witch hunt to me."

"I don't know. What harm could come from disclosing the information? I plan on fully backing his bill, to show my support of transparency in the fracking done by Prescott Oil—or any company for that matter—involved in this type of business."

"Ah, excellent political move, my dear. It also shows you're environmentally friendly."

Jane scowled. "It's more than that, Luke."

"Now, now Jane. Don't be upset. I'm only teasing you. I know your discomfort with the politics of it all. However, I fear your support of this bill would do more harm than good for the people in Texas."

"And why is that?"

Luke leaned over, picked up the cup of coffee, and took a sip before continuing. "If Prescott Oil were forced into full disclosure, then our competitors would have full access to our proprietary business information. This could severely impact our profits. We might have to pull out of Texas."

He took another sip, his eyes observing her over the cup as if gauging her reaction.

She felt like the wind had been knocked out of her. Was he threatening her?

"What exactly do you mean?" She drawled the words slowly.

He carefully placed the cup back on the table and studied her for a moment. "Prescott Oil has brought many jobs to the people of Texas—to people who've been hit during these troubling economic times. It would be a shame if they lost their livelihood because the company had to look elsewhere for a more...amenable location."

Jane's stomach churned. She didn't like where the conversation was going. In all the time she'd known Luke, he'd never interfered with her political work, and he'd never asked for political favors, which she knew were common in the world of politics. So far, most of what she'd done had benefitted the people in her state. The last bill she co-wrote had broken the red tape and allowed companies like Prescott Oil to expand fracking. She was proud of the fact that now it would be easier to bring fracking to more rural counties in the country and even to go international. It would mean more jobs and hopefully a better economy for all. While she was writing the bill, she got a lot of heat from the media, claiming her friendship with Luke had influenced her. It couldn't have been further from the truth.

"Sir, may I have a word with you?"

Jane jumped at the sound of Sal's voice. She looked over at the hulking body at the entrance, taking up the entire doorway. How could someone so huge not make a sound? She wondered how many conversations Sal had overheard between her and Luke over the years.

"What is it, Sal?" Luke's voice sounded irritated. He continued to look at Jane expectantly.

"It's about the Houston transfers in the job-training program. I have the report for you. You said you wanted it as soon as I received it." He held out a manila folder.

"Job-training program?" She raised a brow.

Luke reached out to take the file from him. "It's a program Prescott Oil started about a year ago to train men and women to be ready to work in the oil and gas industry. We have a few transfers from our Houston training site working in Gardenville."

"Really? I'm impressed." Relief swept over her. This was the Luke she knew and loved.

"Prescott Oil is not in it all for the money." Luke glanced down at the report, and a look of disappointment crossed his face. "I have some business to take care of. Think about what I said?"

She looked into his eyes as they gazed back at her kindly. Those were the eyes she remembered from her childhood. Over the past year, she had seen less and less of them, and she wondered what was going on with him to have changed so much. He had always been on her side, and she wanted to trust him like she always had. But lately, she felt like it would be safer for her to keep her thoughts to herself. She couldn't get rid of the nagging feeling that something was off. He was different.

"I'll consider any avenues that benefit the people and our country," she said.

He stood and placed a hand on her shoulder. It was cold.

"That's all I ask."

# 9

Naomi watched Megan climb out of the red pickup truck that was parked along a farm road. She looked exactly the same as when she'd last seen Megan—with her arms and perfect body all over Lash. Same silky blonde hair. Same flawless sun-kissed skin. Same dazzling smile.

Megan smoothed down her pastel yellow dress, flashing manicured nails and matching nail polish.

*Great. Even her nails are gorgeous.* Naomi made a guttural sound in her throat.

Jeremy looked at Naomi curiously. "Anything wrong?"

*Crap! He heard.*

"No. Nothing. Everything's fine," she said, her eyes wide with innocence.

Good grief. Who knew angels could feel things like anger and jealousy? That was something she'd never heard of. She'd always thought they were perfect. Meeting Lash had of course changed that theory and tossed it out the window. And now that she was an angel, she didn't feel any different.

She turned her attention back to Megan, who was leaning into the truck holding her arms out. A little girl, no more than four years old, climbed into them.

"Megan, can you open this for me?" The girl waved what looked like a candy bar in her hand.

"Not now, Emma," said a woman who was the spitting image of the little girl. She grabbed her mass of fiery hair and pulled it up into a ponytail. "You'll get chocolate all over your dress."

"I won't," Emma's pink lips pouted. "I'm a big girl."

Megan smoothed back Emma's unruly ginger curls. "Yes, you are, and you're growing up so fast. But your momma's right. We don't want you to accidentally get candy all over your pretty face before we get your picture taken, do we?"

"Oh, all right," Emma said as Megan placed her on the ground. "Can Teddy be in the picture?"

"Of course." Megan poked her head back into the truck and took out a stuffed bear. "Aunt Verna, where do you want us to sit?"

Naomi sighed as Megan's aunt gave directions on where to sit in the sea of bluebonnets. She remembered the springtime Texas tradition of taking family photos with the pretty blue wildflowers. When she and Chuy were small, Welita and her parents would drive them out to a meadow not too different from this one and have them pose in their church clothes. At the time, she had hated it: having to put on a scratchy dress and then having to deal with Chuy, who teased her. For some reason, Welita thought that wearing a velvet dress in the Texas heat was a good thing.

She always got back at Chuy though. She'd show his friends the photos of him in his little suit and tie. She even threatened to show his friends a photo Welita had taken when he was a baby. It was one that showed his bare bottom. That seemed to shut him up.

As much as she had hated taking those family photos at the time, she'd give anything to have it all back again.

"Now, Emma, sit on Megan's lap and tilt your head a little bit," Aunt Verna instructed.

"Momma, when is Daddy coming to visit?" She asked.

"He's on the road working. He'll come when he feels like it." Verna cursed under her breath.

Emma's lip trembled. "He's not coming 'cause of the 'vorse."

"Don't worry, Emma." Megan gave her a squeeze. "Divorce or not, he loves *you*. He's just busy working. He's in his big truck traveling through Colorado, remember? He'll come to visit soon."

She bobbed her head and then turned her attention to the bear in her arms.

"Megan, can you read to Teddy later?" Emma clutched her toy close to her chest. "Teddy wants to know what happens to the princess."

"Megan has to work tonight," Aunt Verna said as she looked through the camera lens, snapping photos. "I'll read to you."

"I want Megan. She does all the voices." Emma looked up at Megan. "And Teddy thinks she's pretty."

Megan kissed the top of Emma's head. "I think I can squeeze in a few minutes for my favorite little cousin, and Teddy too."

"Emma, put your head down so I can see ya. Look over this way." Aunt Verna pointed in the direction where she and Jeremy were standing.

Emma's big brown eyes widened as she looked directly at Jeremy. Then she flashed a big smile. "Do you want to be in the picture too?"

Naomi gasped and then she turned to Jeremy, who grinned back at Emma, his dimples flashing. "Is she talking to you?"

"I believe so," he said, waving his fingers hello at Emma.

If she could see Jeremy, then that could only mean one thing. She turned back to the petite red-haired girl.

*No!*

"Please don't tell me that she's your next assignment."

His smile disappeared, and he looked at her sadly. "You know I can't tell you."

"Can you give me a hint?"

He studied her for a moment, blue eyes searching her face. He was so close to her that she could see thick dark lashes that any woman would die for, and a smattering of blond stubble on his strong jaw. His eyes held hers, and for a moment, she felt a strange pull towards him.

He blinked and then looked away, releasing her from the strange spell that held her captive. She let out a breath. *What was that?*

She inched herself away from him carefully, trying to keep her distance and at the same time not wanting to hurt his feelings. Was Lash right about him? Did he have feelings for her?

"We each have our assignments. Let's just focus on those, okay?"

"Sure." She watched him as he turned his attention to Megan and Emma. She was being silly. Obviously, Jeremy didn't want to upset her about the little girl.

"Who are you talking to, Hon?" Megan asked.

"The man with the boots." She lifted the bear's arm and waved it at Jeremy.

"Stop that nonsense, Emma," Aunt Verna said. "I told you 'bout your imaginary friends. You can't have them if ya want to go to school with the other big girls. Dag nabbit! I'm runnin' out of battery. Hold on, girls, while I get another one. Don't move."

Emma sniffled, and tears formed in her eyes.

Megan gave her a squeeze and whispered in her ear. "I see him, too." She waved to the left.

"Not there. He's over there," Emma said, pointing in the opposite direction.

Jeremy chuckled. "Sweet girl."

"Who? Megan?" Naomi asked.

"Yeah. Not that many people like to pretend they can actually see me."

Naomi looked at Megan as she waved in the direction Jeremy was standing, making Emma smile again. Okay, so Megan wasn't that bad. Maybe she even was starting to like her a little. Megan seemed like a natural mom the way she was taking care of Emma. Someone who cared for children couldn't be that bad.

The thought made her feel a little bit better—more angelic.

"I guess you could say—"

Naomi was cut off as squawking birds fled from the nearby trees and took off into the sky. Then a strange feeling hit her, and the hairs on the back of her neck stood up.

She glanced at Jeremy. He was on full alert. His thick arms tensed, ready for action, as if he sensed danger nearby.

"Okay, I'm ready now. What da hell?" Verna lost her footing as the ground shook, and she fell.

"Mommy!" Emma shrieked, jumping out of Megan's lap. "What's happening?"

"No, Emma." Megan gripped her arm and pulled her down. She looked up at the swaying utility poles that lined the road. "Stay here with me."

The ground continued to rumble. Emma clutched Megan's neck and cried into her chest.

"What's happening?" Naomi asked Jeremy.

"Earthquake."

"Earthquake! Texas doesn't have earthquakes."

"Not normally, but over the past few years, they've been increasing in frequency." Jeremy looked at her with a surprised look. "Don't you watch the news?"

"Not lately. I've been busy being chased by fallen angels and demons, you know, little things like that," she snapped.

She watched the electrical wires whip around as the poles swayed. Was this it? Was this the danger that she had to protect Megan from? She bit her lip as she looked worriedly at Emma. She didn't want to see the little girl die.

*Please don't let her be Jeremy's assignment.*

The shaking finally stopped, and she let out a breath of relief. They were safe—for now.

"Aunt Verna! Are you all right?" Megan leapt to her feet and ran to her.

"Lord, have mercy. That sure was somethin'. She took a hold of Megan's arm as she helped her to stand. "Dag nabbit! I broke the lens."

Megan sighed and went back to Emma as Verna fiddled with her broken lens. "It's okay, Hon. Your momma's not hurt, just her camera."

"I heard 'bout earthquakes happenin' over in East Texas out in Timpson. Neva thought we'd get one here," Verna said, tugging out a pack of cigarettes from the front of her jean pocket. Her hands shook as she took one out and lit it.

"Uh, Emma." Megan's lips thinned as she eyed the smoke that wafted near her and Emma. "Go wait in the truck."

"Okay. Come on, Teddy. Don't be scared. I'll take care of you." She squeezed the bear to her chest.

"Oh, wait!" Megan unwrapped the candy bar and handed it to her. "Share it with Teddy. It'll calm him down."

Emma beamed. She then glanced over at Jeremy and looked down at her candy. She curled her tiny finger motioning Megan to lean in.

Megan raised an eyebrow and then bent down.

"Do you think I should give some to the pretty man?" Emma whispered.

"She has good taste." Jeremy grinned, throwing Naomi a glance.

Megan looked over in the direction that Emma was looking. "I don't know. I think he wants you to keep it for you and Teddy."

Emma looked to Jeremy with wide eyes.

"Megan's right," he said to Emma. "You and Teddy should keep it."

Emma gasped at the sound of his voice. She was about to say something when she gave a quick look at her mom and shut her mouth closed. She gave Jeremy a simple nod and turned back to Megan. "Okay!"

Megan kissed her forehead, and Emma ran to the truck with Teddy in one hand and the chocolate bar in the other.

Megan got a hold of Verna and led her away from the truck. "When did the other earthquake happen?"

"I think it was a few months ago. Word is that maybe it has to do with all the drillin' that's been goin' on over there."

"We've got just as much drilling here, too." Megan furrowed her brow with worry. "Was it bad over there?"

"4.8. That's what they said in the news. No one got hurt, though."

"Not yet," Megan muttered.

Verna took a final puff on her cigarette and let the smoke out slowly. "Nothin' we can do 'bout it. Best thing that's ever happened to this town is the drillin'. I'd have lost the house if it wasn't for Prescott Oil buyin' some of my land. They even gave me a job. They're good people."

"I don't know about that."

"You tell her, Megan," Naomi said. Yep, she was starting to really like her now.

Jeremy raised an eyebrow at her.

"What? Can't an angel have an opinion on environmental politics?"

He shook his head and chuckled. "You're one of a kind, Naomi."

"No guessing 'bout it." Verna said loudly. She walked to the road and flicked the cigarette, putting it out with her shoe. "It's what puts food on the table and a house over our heads. It's gettin' late, and you need to get ready for your shift at the Dixie Bar tonight."

Jeremy turned to Naomi, his eyes dancing with amusement. "Dixie Bar?"

"Welcome to Texas," she said.

"How long do you think we need to stay?" Naomi said as she watched Megan in a tight-fitting white T-shirt and jean shorts that barely covered her assets, serving customers at the Dixie Bar.

"Why? I'm having fun." His eyes looked appreciatively at Megan.

Naomi rolled her eyes. Just when she was beginning to like Megan, thinking that she had a good head on her shoulders, she acted like...like a blond bimbo.

She gritted her teeth, hating to even think such negative thoughts about the girl she was supposed to be protecting. She couldn't help it. All she could remember was the way her body had rubbed up against Lash's.

Megan moved toward the bar with a tray full of empty beer bottles. Eyes were glued on her as she passed each table. Some whistled at her; others gave her a friendly hello. She smiled and talked to each one.

"What's with the scowl?" Jeremy nudged her.

"I'm not scowling."

He slid his finger down the front of her forehead. "You're telling me this line here is permanent?"

"Not funny, Jeremy." He chuckled as she batted his hand away. "We've been here for hours. I don't think anything is going to happen. She'll continue to be eye candy for all the guys here."

"It's probably best to wait until she's safe in her home," Jeremy said.

Megan was headed in their direction with a tray of burgers. She stopped at a table with a couple of guys, both wearing their Stetsons, typical Texas cowboys. One of them looked like he was stuck in the 70s, with a huge mustache and polyester shirt exposing a hairy chest. She set the tray down and flashed one of her teen-model smiles. When she turned, mustache-man slapped her butt.

Megan's nostrils flared, and her eyes tensed with anger, catching Naomi by surprise.

Quickly smoothing her face, she turned to mustache-man and giggled.

"Now, now." She wiggled her finger at him. "Don't handle the merchandise." She then went to the bar, laid her tray on the counter, and headed straight for the Ladies' room.

*She's acting,* Naomi thought. She didn't like the way she was being treated, but she put up with it anyway. Why would she do that?

A few minutes later, Megan came out of the ladies' room, brushing her fingers under red-rimmed eyes. She took a deep breath and picked up another tray of drinks from the bar.

Naomi finally understood and was actually starting to respect Megan and all she was putting up with in the bar.

If it were her, she'd have chewed out mustache-man and slapped him. Megan had to put up with it. It was a job.

"I'm an idiot," she mumbled under a breath. All Megan was doing was trying to earn a living, and here she was judging her. Some angel she was.

"Aw, Naomi, you're not an idiot," Jeremy said. "You're just a little...misled by the green-eyed monster."

Her eyes shot up at him. "You can read minds, too?"

He smiled. "No. But I'm really good at reading pretty faces...like yours. You have absolutely nothing to be jealous about."

She felt herself grow warm as Jeremy continued to stare at her. This was not good. Not good at all. She needed to get some space between them.

"Well, if we can't leave, can we at least wait outside?" She was headed toward the door when her eyes suddenly grew wide, and she froze.

Jeremy was immediately by her side. "What's wrong?"

She swallowed thickly as she stared at the familiar face that stood at the bar's entrance.

"Chuy," she breathed.

# 10

Lash watched the white and pink petals dancing in the air as he sat beneath one of the cherry trees. Any other day, he would've found the scene enchanting—not today. All he could think about was Naomi. It had been only minutes since she left with Jeremy, but each second that passed felt like an eternity. He was being melodramatic, and he knew it. But he couldn't help himself. Every time he closed his eyes, all he could see was the hurt on her face. And then, when she left, she couldn't even look at him long enough to say good-bye.

"Lash," a soft voice woke him from his thoughts.

He blinked until his eyes focused on Rachel, who stood in front of him with sad eyes. "Oh, hey, Rachel."

"Mind if I join you?"

He shook his head. "I'm not really in the mood for talking."

"Sometimes talking helps," she said, sitting beside him, tucking her legs beneath her. "Raphael told me what happened...about you telling Naomi."

"Who else knows?" The last thing he needed was other angels talking about him. He didn't like the thought of his life being a soap opera for them.

"No, just me...and Michael"—she looked down, fiddling with a blade of grass—"and Gabrielle."

"That's just great. Now everyone knows!"

"Not everyone."

Brown eyes glanced up at him, and he narrowed his eyes. He knew her too well. "And..."

She swallowed. "Well, I may have told Uri."

He groaned. "So all the archangels know I was dumped."

"You were not dumped. Naomi just needs time to think this through."

He let out a loud breath in frustration. He wished he could be patient. It was so hard, especially with her gone—and with Jeremy!

He groaned as he tilted his head back, leaning it against the tree. White blossoms fluttered on a breeze going through the gardens. Some tore off from the branches and sailed to the ground, so delicate, so beautiful, just like Naomi.

"She couldn't even look at me, Rachel. She went on assignment with Jeremy for who knows how long, and she didn't say a word. It's like she gave up on me."

"Don't think like that! She loves you so much. Anyone can see that."

Lash watched a cloud between the branches as it drifted across the sky, covering the sun for a moment and leaving them in a shadow. That's how he felt at that moment—a shadow of himself, empty without Naomi's love.

"I don't know. Maybe there was a reason why we were prevented from being together the first time around. Maybe she's meant to be with someone else." Naomi placing her hand in Jeremy's right before she left was seared in his mind.

"Lash, stop it!" She shook his shoulders, hard. "Snap out of it, and stop talking nonsense."

She moved directly in front of him and reached over, curling her hand behind his neck. "Look at me."

He slowly tilted his head down and looked into determined brown eyes. "I know you don't remember the first time you were with Naomi, and someday I hope you will. But I was there. I know. The love between the two of you was so pure, so beautiful, it broke my heart to see you two being torn apart."

"You're just saying that to make me feel better."

"Argh! I am not. How can I make you believe me?"

"It's okay, Rachel. You've always been a good friend." He took her hand, kissed it, and stood. "If anyone is looking for me, I'll be in the Hall of Judgment." It was nice and dark there. At least there, he'd be left alone.

She let out a growl of frustration and jumped to her feet. Before he knew what was happening, her petite hands jerked his head down and she placed a palm on his temple.

"Hizaher," she whispered the Hebrew command to remember in his ear.

A memory flashed through Lash's mind. He found himself on a familiar hill next to Naomi. She turned to him, her eyes filled with tears as she reached out to cup his face. "I care not if my father has promised me in marriage to Jeremiel. My love for you will never die."

"My sweet Naomi. Your love gives me strength." Lash placed his hands over hers, turned his head, and kissed her palms. "I will plead with my father to allow me to have your hand in marriage. I care not what he does with me so long as I can be with you."

"And if he says no?"

"Then we shall leave this place. Will you go with me? Can you leave your sisters, your family, and join me?"

"Yes. I cannot bear to be without you."

"Then I shall fight for you. I'll never stop fighting for you."

"Nor I you."

Lash gasped as Rachel pulled her hands away. He blinked down at her. "Was that a memory?"

She glanced around the garden with a worried look. "Please don't tell anyone I did that."

Of all the memories he'd been shown of his past, this one was the most vivid. He could feel it to the core of his soul as he if were actually there. He could feel the strength of Naomi's love. She was willing to sacrifice everything to be with him. Not Jeremy. Him!

He scooped Rachel into his arms, lifting her off her feet, and swung her around. "Thank you, Rachel! That was the best gift anyone has ever given me." He set her on the ground and held her tightly against his chest in a bear hug.

"Yohwocom."

"What?" He laughed at the muffled sound she was making and let go of her.

She brushed back her hair and let out a breath. "I said 'you're welcome.' Sometimes, you don't know your own strength. You're pretty strong for a seraph, you know."

"Sorry." He grinned.

"Feeling better now?"

"A little. I mean, it helps to know how much she loved me."

"Loves. Present tense, Lash."

"Okay, *loves*. But she's still mad at me. I hate leaving things like this."

"She'll be back. In the meantime, you just need to keep yourself distracted while she's gone."

She furrowed her brow in thought and then her face lit up. "I know! I'm going to send Uri to you." She slapped a hand on his shoulder. "Get ready for a poker night—Uri style."

A pair of clear blue eyes gazed intently at Lash. "I don't think you have it," Uri said with a thick Russian accent.

"Maybe I do, and maybe I don't." Lash reached for the bottle of vodka, a smuggled gift from Uri, and poured himself a drink. Keeping his eyes on him, he downed it and placed the glass down on the table. "Care to make this interesting?"

Uri's clean-shaven face lit up. "Now you're talking, my friend. What's your price?"

"Cuban cigars." Lash poured himself another drink and brought the glass up to his lips.

"Don't you already have a stash?"

"Raphael found them when he was helping us move," he grumbled.

Uri chuckled.

Lash threw him a glare.

"Say no more." Uri stared down at his cards, his lip twitching.

He shook his head, taking another sip. "What's your price?"

Uri looked up and thought for a moment. "Umm. Okay, Mr. Mister."

Lash choked on his drink and coughed, laughing. "Why are you calling me mister?"

"I'm not calling you mister. I said I want Mr. Mister."

"Uh, okay, so you want a mister?" He furrowed his brow. "What about Rachel?"

Uri looked at him wide-eyed. "It's *for* Rachel."

"For Rachel?" Maybe he didn't know Rachel as well as he thought he did.

"Mr. Mister is an 80s pop rock band. Don't you remember?"

Lash shook his head. There was a lot about the 80s he didn't want to remember.

"She loves their Broken Wings song," he continued. "It's our song. When she was on assignment with me in '86, she played it over and over on an old record player."

"Oh! A record." He was relieved. For a moment there, he thought he was going to be responsible for getting Rachel kicked out. "Well, that might be a little tough to get now-a-days, but I think I can manage."

Uri tilted his head. "What did you think I was talking about?"

"Nothing." His eyes darted to his cards. "Okay, what do you have?"

"Royal flush."

"Shit!"

Uri howled as he leaned over the table and poured himself a drink. "Don't tell Rachel. I want to surprise her."

"No problem there. I don't know when I'll be able to get it for you though. It doesn't look like I'm going down anytime soon." Lash pushed himself away from the table, and taking the bottle with him, he went to the large window that overlooked the valley below.

"Care for another game?"

Lash pressed his forehead against the glass. It was no use. Even the wisecracking Uri couldn't keep his heart from aching over Naomi. He'd been so happy when Rachel showed him that memory of Naomi giving up everything just for him, proof of her love for him. He wished he could just hold on to it. Instead, every time he closed his eyes, all he could see was the hurt on her face. Eyes that once looked at him with tender love were glazed over in pain and betrayal, eyes that wouldn't even look at him when she left. Had he gone too far? Had he lost her love?

"It's no good, Uri. Thanks for trying. It's just...I can't get her out of my mind."

He heard the sound of cards shuffling as he looked at the bridge, wondering if he would be able to find her if he looked. Maybe he could sneak over there in the morning.

"You don't remember this, but long ago, I was a royal ass-hole."

Lash spun around, taken off guard. "Did you say ass-hole?"

Uri stared out into space as he shuffled the cards deftly in his fingers. "I didn't deserve the love Rachel gave to me. I knew she cared, and I took advantage. I didn't know what a gift she was until she came after me, and then it was too late. When I returned centuries later as a human, she was there again. Of course, I didn't know her at first. I kept having these strange feelings whenever she was around. What do you call it?"

He paused for a moment then snapped his fingers. "Déjà vu. It was like I knew her before in another life. Then, I fell in love with her. I couldn't help myself. By then, the tables were turned, and she kept her heart away from me. Oh, she watched over me; that was her job, but never would she let me in. I know now it was because of how I treated her in the past."

Lash stayed silent. This was the first time he'd ever seen Uri so serious. Rachel never talked about their past. In his mind, they were the perfect couple, forever loyal to each other and deeply in love.

Uri placed the cards on the table and looked at him with determination in his eyes. "I had to fight to win back Rachel's trust. That is what you must do, my friend. Fight for your woman."

"You think I don't want to do that? I'm stuck here waiting for her."

Uri pushed himself away from the table and went to him, slapping a hand down on his shoulder. "Then you will go to her. I'm giving you permission to go down and find her."

"What about Gabrielle and Michael?"

"I'll handle that. If you're brief, we may not have to deal with them."

"When can I go?"

"When the moment is right, I'll find you. Be ready."

# 11

"Is it over?" Naomi mumbled from behind hands that she kept over her face. She didn't dare take a peek at what Chuy was doing and risk another wave of nausea like the first time when she saw him flirting with Megan. Who knew angels could get nauseous?

Jeremy chuckled. "Don't you think you're being overdramatic?"

Okay, maybe she was overreacting just a tad bit. When Chuy, closely followed by Lalo, had walked into the bar, she'd been overjoyed. In that moment, she'd completely forgotten she was an angel and not visible to anyone. She'd been so happy, she'd even wanted to hug Lalo. Jeremy had to stop her from running to them, reminding her that she was not human anymore.

Although she was sad that she couldn't talk with Chuy and Lalo, she stood back with Jeremy, happy with the thought that if they were here, then Welita was sure to be nearby. She listened in while they talked about their work at Prescott Oil, hoping to get a clue of where Welita was located.

Then Megan showed up and asked for their order.

"I can't bear to watch this," she said with her hands still over her eyes. She knew she was acting like a dippy teenager, but she couldn't help herself. "It's just so, ugh, so gross. I mean, Chuy making his moves on Megan. It's bad enough I have to hear it."

Jeremy tugged on her hands and pulled them from her face. "He's not that bad."

She dropped her hands and glanced up at him, noting the amused expression on his face. "Seriously?"

"The man's holding his own. He's got some smooth moves." He winked.

She looked over to Chuy, and groaned. He was flexing his bicep for Megan and showing her a tattoo that he had on his right shoulder.

Chuy got a tattoo! When did this happen? He must be nuts doing something like that. If Welita found out, she'd flip out. Probably find a way to remove it herself.

"Ooh, I love it!" Megan said as her fingers brushed over his tanned muscles. "I wish I could get one. Where did you get yours?"

"I got it down in Houston before we moved up here," Chuy said.

"You guys are from Houston? I've never been there."

Chuy leaned in close to her, his voice husky. "Maybe we can take you for a visit sometime. I was planning on going back to get another one next week."

Lalo spit out his beer. "You're going to get another one after Welita tore you apart for getting the first one?"

Naomi burst out laughing at the look on Chuy's face.

"Not now, Lalo," Chuy hissed.

Megan raised an eyebrow. "Welita? Who's that?"

"Chuy's grandmother." Lalo picked up a nacho chip and put a jalapeño on top of it. "She moved up here with us." He popped the chip into his mouth.

"You live with your grandmother?"

Lalo held his hand up as he chewed quickly before answering her. "Chuy lived with her in Houston, but after her heart attack, we had to move up here to work."

Sweat beaded on Lalo's forehead, and he took a swig of beer. "She's in an assisted-living complex near our apartment."

Naomi took a step forward, hoping that he would say the name of the place Welita was staying.

"Oh, that's so sad. Is she all right?" Megan asked.

"Yep, she's good." Lalo picked up a chip and pointed it at Chuy. "Good enough to whip your ass if you get another tattoo." He grinned.

Chuy groaned.

*Love ya, Lalo!* Naomi thought.

"Aw, that's so sweet," Megan purred as she batted her thick lashes. "I like that...taking care of your grandmother like that. Where do you work?"

Chuy threw Lalo a glance and then turned to Megan with a smile. "Prescott Oil. We're in their job-training program."

Her green eyes widened. "You guys are engineers?"

Lalo wiped a napkin over his forehead. "Nah, they have me doing janitorial work in one of the offices. But Chuy, they have him working on the wells, and—"

The glasses and beer bottles on the table trembled.

"What's that?" The bartender asked, trying to keep the glasses from falling to the floor.

"I think it's an airplane flying overhead," a waitress said.

"It's happening again." Jeremy glanced at Naomi, his face furrowed with worry.

"Do you know anything about this?"

He shook his head. "I was only told about my assignment. It's not difficult to figure out where this could lead to, though."

The shaking grew more violent. People started screaming and running toward the exit.

Naomi watched Chuy catch Megan when she lost her balance and then help her to the door. She followed them closely, thankful that she was near Chuy and Lalo and could make sure they were okay. She hoped Welita was safe, wherever she was.

As soon as they stepped outside the bar, the trembling stopped.

"Are you okay?" Chuy kept his arm around Megan.

"Yes, I'm fine." The flirtatiousness in her voice was gone, and her face grew serious. "I-I need to get home."

"I'll walk you to your car. Where is it?"

"My truck's over there." She pointed to across the lot.

When they reached the truck, Chuy and Lalo stood off to the side as she tried to start it.

"Damn it!" She slapped the steering wheel when the engine didn't turn over.

"Hold on." Chuy popped up the hood and tinkered under it for a few minutes. "Try it again."

She turned the ignition. "Nope. Still nothing."

"Could be the alternator," Lalo said.

"Yeah, it looks like it. Megan, let me take you home. I can fix this up for you in the morning." Chuy closed the hood.

"Oh, I don't want to be a bother. I'll find someone to give me a ride."

"No bother at all." Chuy grinned. "Lalo, I'll leave you off at Sunrise Haven. Look in on Welita, and let her know I'm helping out a friend."

Naomi stood in the middle of the circular drive in front of Sunrise Haven. Welita was in there, somewhere inside that two-story building. She wanted to see her so badly.

It was a nice facility. Paved sidewalks were lined with perfectly trimmed hedges, and there were beds of flowers scattered around the building. There was even a huge porch that wrapped around one side of the wood and brick building. Naomi could imagine Welita sitting in one of the rocking chairs, enjoying the evening sunset and fussing with the landscapers for not feeding the surrounding flowers and plants enough.

When Lalo jumped out of the truck and waved after Chuy and Megan, she watched with deep yearning as he went through the sliding glass doors of the entrance. It took every ounce of strength for her to not run inside.

"Naomi," Jeremy said softly. "We need to go."

"Can't I stay? Just for a few minutes?" The glass doors slid open as a couple walked out. It would only take her a few seconds. She would be quick. Run in and out. She just wanted to make sure Welita was safe.

Jeremy placed himself in front of her, blocking her view of the building. He placed a hand underneath her chin, lifting her head. Blue eyes gazed into hers. "We have jobs to do. If you see her, it'll just make it harder for you to leave. We need to go."

Naomi looked deep into his eyes and saw how much he wanted to let her stay, to give her what she wanted. Then she thought of Lash, and her heart ached. She was still upset with him, but she couldn't help that she needed him, wanted him with her. He would understand.

*No, Jeremy's right.* She had a job to do. She pushed the thought of Lash to the back of her mind, focusing on what was expected of her.

"Okay, let's go."

They caught up with Chuy's truck as it rambled down a rural gravel road. There were no other houses in sight, and she wondered how far from town Megan lived.

After a few minutes, he finally turned the truck onto a dirt path, barely visible from the road. He came to a stop a few yards from a small ranch house with green shutters. The porch was a matching dark green that looked freshly painted. On one side of the porch, a Texas flag hung proudly. A U.S. flag waved on the opposite side.

A few yards to the left of the house were a few cars. Most of them had flat tires. She smiled, thinking how Chuy and her father would love to get their hands on them. They loved to bring old cars back to life.

Naomi took a deep breath, wishing she could turn back time. She missed her parents.

She furrowed her brow as she inhaled a strange odor. "Do you smell that?"

She looked to Jeremy with alarm when he didn't respond. He simply looked down at her with a knowing sad look in his eyes.

Her heart dropped into the pit of her stomach. Whatever it was, he knew, and he wasn't telling her. She tensed, readying herself. Whatever was coming, it was coming soon. She hoped and prayed that Chuy wasn't involved.

She watched carefully as Chuy jumped out of the truck, ran to the door, and opened it. Megan's pink lips curled into a delicate smile.

A breeze blew hard, making the flags flutter wildly. Megan swiped a hand around her hair as it blew wildly in the wind and then tied it into a ponytail.

"Everything looks all right," she said, glancing at the house. "Thank you for everything tonight. You don't have to fix the truck. I can get it towed in the morning."

"I want to. Lalo and I fix up stuff like that all the time. It's simple, really."

"You're sweet." She tapped his muscular chest. Her finger slid down his tight-fitting T-shirt and started outlining his abs. She then looked up at him and smiled.

Chuy reached out and tucked a loosened blonde strand behind her ear. "So are you."

He dipped his head, and his lips gently touched hers. Her hands worked their way up his bulging arms and into his thick hair. A soft moan escaped her as he placed a hand against the small of her back and pressed her against his chest.

The front porch light switched on, and there was the sound of a door slamming.

"Megan, is that you out there?"

They jumped.

"Crap! It's my aunt." Megan stepped away from Chuy. "Yeah, it's me. Are you guys all right?"

"Emma's in her room, sleepin' like a rock." Verna took out a pack of cigarettes and a lighter from the pocket of her robe. "The house could fall down 'round her and she'd still be sleepin'. Nothin' can wake her up once she's down."

"That's good!" Megan yelled back. "I'll be right in!"

Verna placed the cigarette in her mouth. "Take your time." She raised the lighter.

"I should be going," Chuy said as Megan turned back to face him. "I'll call you—"

Naomi heard the flick of Verna's lighter, followed by a loud explosion. She screamed as fire flashed out toward Chuy and Megan.

Chuy threw himself over Megan, sending them both to the ground. Without thought, Naomi rushed to them, her body shielding both from the intense heat.

"Aunt Verna! Oh my God!"

Chuy tightened his grip on Megan, who clawed the ground. His eyes widened at the ball of fire blazing on the side of the porch.

There was another explosion, and flames shot through the windows, sending shards of glass flying through the air. He covered Megan with his body and ducked his head.

"What do I do?" Naomi looked in horror at the spot where Verna was.

Jeremy stood by her, holding her hand. "You're doing it. Just stay with Megan."

"Emma!" Megan cried as she tried to push Chuy off her. "I have to get Emma."

*Emma!*

The thought screamed in Naomi's head and slammed her chest like a sledgehammer. An image of a cute little girl with red hair, freckles, and chocolate-stained lips flashed before her eyes. She looked frantically at Jeremy, her eyes wild.

He squeezed her hand, eyes glistening, and shook his head.

"No. Stay here. I'll get her." Chuy scrambled to his feet. "Where is she?"

"Second door on the right. Towards the back of the house. Hurry, please, hurry!" Megan cried.

"Chuy, don't!" Naomi screamed as Chuy leapt to his feet and headed for the burning house.

Jeremy tackled her by the waist when she attempted to run after him.

"Let me go! Let me go! It's Chuy!" She kicked out, trying to escape his grip.

"You can't do this," he grunted as she continued to struggle against him.

"He's my family. Please, please let me go," she cried, tears streaming down her face. He was too strong for her, and he wasn't budging.

Slowly, he turned her to face him. Fiery shadows danced on his tense face. His eyes flicked between her and the house. He brushed the tears from her cheeks with his thumbs and gazed intently into her eyes. "Stay with Megan. Whatever happens, *do not* leave her side."

She nodded as she choked back the lump in her throat and watched Jeremy fly into the house.

Naomi turned at the sound of Megan gasping and crying. She stayed on the ground clutching her stomach and mumbling Emma's name over and over.

Naomi circled Megan, twisting her hands as she fought a war within herself. She was torn between wanting to calm Megan and wanting to run inside the house. She knew it was her job to stay with her. She had been given direct orders. Every fiber of her being wanted to disobey them and go protect Chuy, her own flesh and blood, at any cost. It was eating her up, having to protect the woman she had once loathed and being forbidden to help her own family. She could only hope that Jeremy would help Chuy and Emma.

Naomi inhaled sharply as a sudden thought crossed her mind. *Jeremy is the angel of death. He is in there with Chuy.*

Curling her fingers into fists, she banged them against her thighs. Why hadn't she thought of that before? And she'd let Jeremy go in there! Who was he there for? Chuy? Emma? Maybe it was Megan's aunt.

She glanced at the spot where the older woman lay. She jerked her head away as bile rose in her throat at the sight of the poor woman.

Guilt gnawed deep within her. What kind of angel was she? She couldn't believe she was hoping someone else would die, just so Chuy would be safe.

Sirens screamed in the distance, and she prayed for them to come faster. She stared at the front door, where the flames grew larger.

"Come on, Jeremy. Come out with them. Please come out," Naomi prayed.

Fire engines emerged from the distance. Within minutes, they came to a halt near them.

Megan got up and ran to them. "They're still in there. My Emma is in there! She's just a little girl. Please get her!"

Just as two of the firemen ran into the blazing house, Jeremy stepped out.

Pained eyes locked with hers.

*No! No! No!*

She felt herself failing as the world collapsed around her. Flashing lights of the fire engines shrank into tiny specks of light as the darkness took over. Sirens and the yells of the firefighters merged into one sound that muffled until there was nothing but white noise whistling in her ears. She wheezed, struggling for air as a sea of pain washed over her, drowning her. She reached out, desperate to hold on to something, anything to keep her from falling further into the darkness. A pair of strong arms found her and held on to her tight as she sank to her knees and wept.

# 12

"Place the bags over there," Jane instructed the young man carrying two of her suitcases. "Does Mr. Prescott have the Dallas paper?"

"I'll have it brought to you, Ma'am."

"Thank you," she said as he walked out the door. She should have known Luke would have everything she needed ready for her. Why wouldn't he? The size of his house staff could rival that of all the boutique hotels in the area.

It wasn't the first time she'd stayed in Luke's sprawling Dallas ranch home. Although this time, she would've preferred to stay at a hotel, especially since she was back in Texas specifically to make her announcement to run for president. She was surprised when Luke insisted that she stay with him. He didn't seem at all concerned that the media would accuse him of seeking congressional favors.

She still hadn't decided what to do about Congressman Keith's bill. She had a funny feeling it was why Luke insisted that she make her presidential campaign announcement in Gardenville rather than Austin, the state's capital. He wanted her to see the families who would be impacted by the bill if it passed.

She sighed. Luke had never pressured her like this before. Voting down the bill must be really important to make him act like one of the hundreds of lobbyists who hounded her on a daily basis. It was so unlike him, and she wondered if there was more to it than just business.

Just as she was about to take off her shoes and relax, there was a knock at the door.

She opened the door. "Yes?"

"Mr. Prescott is waiting for you in the library," said a young woman who stood at the entrance. "He would like to go over details of the presidential announcement in Gardenville as soon as possible."

"Of course."

"Oh, and here is the paper you requested." The woman handed her a copy of the Dallas newspaper.

Jane skimmed the headlines. She felt a knot in her stomach when one caught her attention.

*Gas Explosion Kills Gardenville Woman.*

"Ma'am?"

She blinked and looked up at the woman. "Tell Mr. Prescott I'll be there in a moment."

She nodded and closed the door.

Jane pulled out her reading glasses and sank to the plush sofa. Scanning the paper, she inhaled sharply when familiar names appeared.

*A gas explosion in Gardenville, Texas, a small town west of Abilene and the hub of Prescott Oil's hydrofracture drilling, ripped through a home, shaking the nearest neighbors, miles away.*

*The blast instantly killed the homeowner, Verna Dalene, 45. Emma Dalene, 4, was seriously injured and taken to a nearby hospital for burn injuries and smoke inhalation. Megan Dalene, 21, and Chuy Duran, 23, were treated for smoke inhalation and released.*

*Authorities reported that the explosion may have been caused by a gas leak after a gas line in the home was damaged. One authority noted that a recent string of earthquakes has caused cracks in underground pipes and gas lines.*

*Residents in the community suspect that the quakes are linked to the recent fracking in the area and are calling for local officials to investigate Prescott Oil.*

*Billionaire Luke Prescott is well known for his ties to Senator Jane Sutherland, who will be formally announcing her presidential campaign in Gardenville on Friday.*

She folded the paper, tucked it under her arm, and headed out of her room toward the library. As she walked down the stairs, she wondered if Luke knew anything about this and if maybe they should move to a different location for their announcement. Or maybe postpone.

And the name...Chuy Duran. It couldn't be the same Durans. Could it? It was too much of a coincidence. Maybe Luke could have Sal look into it.

When she was a few feet from the library, she heard muffled voices arguing. She stopped outside the door, shocked when she recognized Sal's harsh, baritone voice. She'd never heard him raise his voice at Luke before. Something was wrong.

"How can you be so sure she'll make an appearance?" Sal's voice drifted down the hall.

"Do not forget, Saleos. The girl's greatest weakness is her love for her family," Luke said. "She is so much like Raphael."

*Raphael? Who's Raphael?*

Luke shared a lot of his business contacts with her, often giving her little bit of gossip to amuse her during boring social functions she had to attend in Washington. She didn't recall anyone named Raphael. And why was Luke calling Sal 'Saleos'? Was that his real name? Strange.

"You're taking much risk going after that one. We should focus on the plan to increase the company's investments so that we can take Prescott Oil global. Without it, you'll not be able to rise in power. As we speak, Michael is gathering forces."

"It's a risk worth taking," Luke snapped. "Your job is to make sure that the Durans stay put, and see to it that they're not put in harm's way until the girl is here."

Jane gasped. The Durans! It wasn't a coincidence. It was Anita Duran's grandson who was in the paper.

Why was Luke bothering that poor family, especially after the girl, Naomi, disappeared in the desert a year ago? She wondered what he was hiding and why. Why would he do something like that? She remembered asking him about the boy, Javier Duran. Could it be that he lied to her?

She shook her head. None of this was making sense. What did Sal mean about Luke's rise in power? Luke was already a powerful man with his vast amount of financial resources. She knew he wanted to expand fracking into third-world countries. He was also expanding into water exploration. Was this Michael who Sal mentioned a business competitor?

"I've checked the hospital. The boy called Chuy suffered no injuries, other than smoke inhalation."

"Good, make sure he and his grandmother stay out of trouble."

Sal laughed.

"Do you find anything humorous about the situation?"

Sal cleared his throat. "Don't you? It was the quake that created the leak in the gas pipes that eventually led to the explosion. Do you think Michael placed Megan Dalene in Chuy's path?"

"That would be very unlikely. It would be an act of desperation for Michael to place a human at risk. He has too much *faith*"—Luke sneered the word—"to do something like that. No, I think it was mere coincidence."

"Should I do something about the Dalene girl? There's a lot of media attention on her right now. Your political adversaries may use her against the senator."

"The blonde whore? Who in their right mind would listen to her?" Luke laughed. "I have a copy of her criminal file right here."

After a ruffling of papers, Luke continued. "Arrested for prostitution, in possession of methamphetamine, possession of marijuana, petty theft, and the list goes on. No, this Megan Dalene is not a threat. Let the media have their fun with her. It'll blow over quickly."

Jane heard footsteps down the hall heading in her direction. She quickly walked toward the library, clicking her heels loudly on the wood floor, making sure she was heard and then knocked. "Luke?"

"Ah, Jane, come in, come in."

She entered the library and glanced over at Sal, giving him a slight nod of greeting. His jaw flexed as he clenched his teeth, his head barely making a nod in return.

She blinked and felt a sense of cold wash over her. She took in the way he stood stiff and unmoving. Somehow, he seemed to look bigger, more threatening. Although she was used to his dismissal of her, only acknowledging when it was expected from him, his animosity toward her seemed to have grown within the past few months.

She took in black eyes that pierced through her, the ferocious scowl, and huge muscles that bulged in a snug-fitting black suit. He looked like a hit man. The type of guy one would see in the movies, who mob bosses hired to kill people like...political figures. She shivered at the thought.

"Did you read the Dallas paper?" She waved the paper at Luke.

"Yes. What a shame."

Jane studied his face. For the first time, she noticed his gray eyes looked empty, void of emotion, even though his words sounded sincere. "I was thinking we could put together a small fundraiser for the family."

"My dear Jane," he took the paper from her and placed a hand on her shoulder. "I do admire your compassion. However, it's not a good idea to do so at this time. We don't want to draw attention away from your announcement."

"We have to do something. And the poor little girl, she's fighting for her life. If Prescott Oil is to blame, we need to make this right, Luke."

Anger flashed across his face. His hand seared her shoulder as if it was on fire. She winced, taking a small step away from him.

In a blink, his face was back to normal, as if she had imagined it. His lips curled into a smile that caused the hairs on the back of her neck to stand. "I've already made some phone calls, and there's a full investigation underway as we speak. I'll send Sal to set up an *anonymous* donation to the family."

He crumpled the paper and tossed it into the trash. "There. Done. Now, shall we go over the key points in your speech?"

Jane was shocked by the way he took over. He'd never done that before. He was definitely hiding something from her.

She glanced over at Sal and then back at Luke. Both were watching her expectantly, as if wondering what her next move would be. A voice screamed inside of her, warning her not to press the issue with him. That same voice warned her that it would be dangerous for her to do so.

She'd stop for now, but she wasn't letting go. Somehow, she was going to get to the bottom of this. She'd find out, one way or another, what was going on. And the place to start was to find and talk to Anita Duran.

# 13

Naomi brushed the tears from her cheek with the back of her hand as she watched Megan read to a sleeping Emma. It broke her heart to see the little girl in the hospital bed, her tiny body lying in a sea of white: white bandages around her arms and hands, white sheets and pillows, and the white walls of the hospital.

Naomi alternated between feeling heartbroken for Emma and elated that Chuy was alive. She hadn't believed Jeremy when he told her Chuy was still alive until she'd seen him, limping out of the house with a fireman under his arm, helping him.

She had cried into Jeremy's chest, relieved, until another fireman came out with Emma in his arms. Pain had crossed over Jeremy's face, and she had realized that the look he'd given her when he first came out was because of Emma.

Chuy sat in the corner of the room, taking turns with Megan reading all of Emma's favorite stories. Naomi wasn't surprised that he had stayed with them, even though he had just met Megan. He was always the first person to volunteer to help a neighbor when it was needed. And when it came to children, he was putty in their hands.

Chuy had held onto Megan when the doctor told her that her aunt died. Naomi could tell Megan already knew her aunt was dead. There was something about hearing it from someone else that somehow made it more real. She knew what it was like, and so did Chuy.

He even helped her by contacting her aunt's ex-husband, who was driving in from North Dakota. When he read a Berenstain Bears book to Emma, Megan asked him to do voices as he read. Naomi couldn't help but smile when his voice went up three octaves when he read the momma bear's part.

"I hope she's not in pain," Naomi said as she watched Emma's little chest rise and fall. "Do you think she can feel anything?"

"I don't think so." Jeremy's voice was somber as he also focused his attention on Emma. "I've been doing this for a long time. I must have taken hundreds of children to the other side. I still can't get used to it."

"Really?"

He looked down at her, his eyes sad. "Yeah. They're so full of life, so trusting."

Naomi glanced over at Chuy just as his hands gently brushed back Emma's hair out of her face, and she thought of Welita. She wondered how Welita was reacting to Chuy almost getting killed. She hadn't been able to follow Chuy when he left the hospital briefly to visit Welita. Knowing Chuy, he probably hadn't told her, or if he had, he'd played it down.

The thought that Chuy could have died, leaving Welita all alone, tore her heart. If only she could see her, somehow she would let her know that she was watching over her.

"Naomi?" Jeremy placed an arm around her shoulder. "What is it?"

She looked up into blue eyes that looked at her tenderly. "I need to see my grandmother. Please," she breathed.

He held her eyes for a moment and then pulled her to him, pressing her against his chest. She heard his heart pounding frantically. She knew she should pull away, but she couldn't help herself. She felt so alone, and he was her friend.

Lips pressed against the top of her head, and he sighed. "I know it's been hard for you. I'll find a way for you to see her."

She squeezed him tight. "Thank you."

When she looked up at him, the raw emotion on his face took her breath away. Intense eyes searched her face and then rested on her lips. Slowly, he ducked his head, lips parting.

A voice inside her told her to let go, step away.

"I can't stand this anymore!"

Jeremy jumped at the sound of Megan's voice.

Naomi pulled back and watched Megan as she rose from her chair and paced the room.

*That was close.* She couldn't let that happen again.

"Why don't you go outside and get some fresh air?" Chuy said, placing the book down on his lap. "I'll stay with her until you come back."

"No, it's not that." She pressed her hands against her forehead and shut her eyes. "It's just that this didn't have to happen. If we weren't getting all these quakes, the pipes would've never gotten damaged, and Aunt Verna would still be here, and Emma...Emma would..."

Red blotches appeared on her face and she choked on tears.

Chuy immediately stood up and wrapped his arms around her.

She sobbed into his chest. "It's not right. This shouldn't have happened."

"Megan, you've been here twenty-four hours straight. You need to get some sleep. You'll feel better," he said as he rubbed her back, trying to soothe her.

She shook her head. "No, I can't just sit back and let them get away with this. All my life I've been pushed around. I never fought back because I thought I deserved it. I thought I was nothing. I'm not nothing. I *am* somebody."

"Of course you are. What do you want to do?"

Megan sniffed. "I want to take Prescott Oil down. I just know this is happening because of all the fracking they're doing. It's messing up the land somehow. I even heard that they're putting something in the water."

"I don't know, Megan." He brushed a hand through his thick hair. "People have been saying that for years. There are entire organizations that have tried to bring them down. No one can touch them, and they're gonna keep growing."

Megan shook her head. "I don't care. I'll find a way. I'll go to the media. Wait a minute." She paused, furrowing her brow, deep in thought. Then her eyes widened, and she snapped her fingers. "You work for them. Maybe you can find out what they're doing. I'm sure they're doing things illegally."

"I can't do that. I don't want to lose my job."

"You still want to work for them? Emma doesn't have a mother anymore because of them."

"You don't understand, Megan." His voice was somber. "I have to take care of my family."

"You could've died too, Chuy! Who would've taken care of your family then? I bet you wouldn't go back to work for them if Prescott Oil killed your family."

Naomi's breath hitched as she watched Chuy's brown eyes darken and his nostrils flare. His voice was low and steady as he looked intently at Megan. "I lost my uncle when Jane Sutherland killed him in a car accident. My cousin tried fighting back, and days later, she disappeared."

"Oh, Chuy," Naomi whispered as she felt tears stinging her eyes.

"I know she's dead. I felt it the moment it happened. It was like a part of me disappeared that day." His voice was thick. "I can't help but think that somehow Luke Prescott was involved in all of it."

Megan placed a hand on his arm, speaking softly. "Then how can you still work for them?"

"I have no choice!" He spun around and headed toward the window. Looking out with his back to her, he said, "They took everything away from us. Everything! I couldn't get a job anywhere."

Megan went to him and placed a hand on his back. "I'm so sorry."

He turned to face her. "Believe me, I tried. I got a lot of interviews, but every time I showed up, it was like suddenly the job was no longer available. The only one who offered me work was the Prescott Oil training program. I didn't even apply for it! I got a letter offering me a job. Lalo got the same letter two days later. We thought it was offered to everyone who lived in the neighborhoods that were bought out by the company."

Chuy sank into the chair under the windowsill and dropped his head into his hands. "I sold out. I didn't know what to do. I'm sorry, Naomi. I'm so sorry. I didn't know what to do. God, I wish I had her strength."

Tears streamed down Naomi's face as she went to Chuy. She placed a hand on his head, wishing he could feel

---

her. "It's okay, Chuy. I'm sorry I wasn't there to help. I'm here for you now."

Chuy lifted his head and looked around.

"What is it?" Megan asked.

He tilted his head as if listening.

Naomi's eyes widened, and she looked to Jeremy. "Can he hear me?"

"It's doubtful, but I think he can sense you," he replied.

After a moment, Chuy shook his head. "Never mind." He took a deep breath and reached for Megan's hand. "Look, I know if Naomi were still here, she'd want me to help you."

Her face lit up. "Will you?"

"Yeah, but we only have a brief window to do this. All Prescott Oil employees were given time off to attend the senator's presidential campaign announcement Friday. You can get national media coverage there."

"I don't have any proof to expose them, or anything that will at least get the feds to investigate them."

Chuy stood and reached for his cell phone. "Yeah, let me give Lalo a call."

"Lalo?" Megan and Naomi voiced at the same time.

"They have him doing janitorial work in the offices where they keep confidential information. He can get into their servers and dig up some information for us."

"He can?" Megan and Naomi said in unison.

Chuy grinned. "Lalo has mad computer skills that would make even Mark Zuckerberg drool."

# 14

Naomi stood at the entrance of Sunrise Haven. She couldn't believe that in a few minutes, she would be with Welita again.

"Nervous?"

Jeremy looked down at her with the same tender expression that he had at the hospital. She didn't know what to do about it, especially now, when he was going against protocol and allowing her to see Welita. She owed him so much. She didn't want to hurt him.

"A little."

She felt a quiet calm when he placed a hand on her cheek. "Want me to go in there with you?"

She gazed into his eyes and saw the love he had for her. He cared...too much. She turned her head and took a step back, feeling a stab of pain when she did so. She hated hurting him this way after he'd been so kind to her.

"No. I'll be fine."

"It doesn't look like Megan will be leaving the hospital anytime soon, and Chuy is with Lalo. I'll watch over Megan for you, so take your time."

He turned and started to walk away.

"Jeremy." She grasped hold of his arm before he could leave. "Thanks for letting me do this."

She watched his broad shoulders stiffen at her touch. When he turned back to face her, his face was somber. His eyes held hers for a moment, and he swallowed. Then his face shifted, erasing the pained expression and putting on his normal, flirtatious twinkle. "Let's just call it my gift to my future sister."

He winked, and then he was gone.

Naomi closed her eyes and sighed. It was going to be more difficult than she thought, working so closely with Jeremy. She loved Jeremy; he was so sweet and caring. She wanted so much to be close to him, like a true sister. Maybe if she had a talk with him, aired it all out in the open, they could find a way to be like family, without all the awkwardness.

*I'll have a talk with him when the assignment is over.* Now, she needed to see Welita.

She headed toward the glass doors, and they slid open as she approached. She really didn't have to use the entrance. It was a habit. She still couldn't get used to being an angel. She could've easily just made herself appear anywhere in the building, although she didn't know exactly which room Welita was in.

She glided down the halls, listening carefully for any signs of where Welita might be. She heard the muffled sounds of women talking to each other and dishes clattering. In one room, she heard an older woman cooing and the sounds of a baby giggling, making her smile. She thought about going into the room so she could see, but then thought against it, reminding herself that she shouldn't abuse her angelic abilities. The family in the room that the happy noises were coming from deserved their privacy.

In that moment, she realized Welita would never have a chance to hold her child, and the thought saddened her.

Then she heard a loud and familiar voice that chased the thought away.

"Ay, Dios mio! No, Pablo! Don't listen to her. She's lying to you. Maria slept with your brother. She's carrying his child, not yours."

Naomi chuckled at Welita, yelling at the television. She always did that when she was watching her favorite show—a telenovela about Pablo Rivera, the handsome ranch owner, and Maria, his maid turned movie actress.

She followed Welita's voice until she found the place it was coming from. She stepped into the room, and her hand flew to her mouth, stifling a cry, when she saw Welita sitting on a small sofa. Her brown wrinkled hands stroked Bear's fur while she stared intently at the TV screen.

"Oh, Welita," Naomi sobbed. "What's happened to you?"

Welita's raven hair was now almost entirely white. Her once-strong hands were like brown toothpicks, ready to break at the slightest touch. She was so frail. It was as if the life in her that made her rock solid had been zapped away, leaving her a shell of who she once was.

Naomi's eyes shifted to the walker beside the chair. She must've been really bad off to even allow something like that in her presence. Welita had always been so proud to be independent and to use her own two feet to get around.

*I did this to her.* If she had been there, she could have helped Chuy get Welita the best health care so that she would've never needed the walker in the first place.

Better yet, if she had stayed with her and never left with Lash, Welita would've never had a heart attack. She would still have her home. She'd be watching Pablo and Maria in her own living room in Houston, not in some one-bedroom apartment in an assisted-living home in North Texas.

Naomi took a step closer. Bear's head jolted up; her ears perked straight up like two furry antennae, and she barked.

"Not now, Bear." Welita patted Bear's head. "Wait for the commercial."

Bear's brown eyes looked straight at Naomi.

"Can you see me, Girl?" Maybe she could. She recalled Lash saying that sometimes animals could see angels.

Bear sniffed the air and then leapt off Welita's lap, yapping. She ran in circles around Naomi's feet, whining, as if she were crying. Her tail wagged so fast, it was a blur.

"Oh my God! You can see me! I missed you too." She laughed as she reached down to pet her. Her hand went through Bear's body, and Bear shivered. "I'm sorry, Girl. I wish I could touch you."

"Ay, Bear! Why are you crying? I'll let you out during the commer—"

Naomi watched as Welita turned slowly in the direction where she stood. "Who's there?"

"It's me, Welita. Can you see me?" Of course she couldn't. Why should she? Welita was able to see Rebecca, but that was because she had shown herself to Welita. Rebecca was her guardian angel. Naomi wasn't. "I wish you could see me."

Welita closed her eyes and reached up for something on her chest. Naomi went over to her and looked down, wondering what she was doing.

Her hand flew up to her mouth, and she sobbed. It was her necklace. Welita was wearing the necklace Naomi's father had given to her on her graduation night. "Oh Welita, I miss you so much."

Welita opened her eyes. Looking up, she smiled. "Naomi," she breathed.

*She knows! She knows I'm here.* Tears streamed down Naomi's cheeks.

Naomi knelt in front of the sofa, placing her hands over Welita's. If only she could feel her touch, feel the strength of her hands, the hands that always guided her when she was lost, the hands that soothed her when she was in pain, the hands that always reached out to her with unconditional love. "Oh, Welita, there's so much I wish I could tell you. If only...if only..."

The air became a buzz of energy, and she felt a warmth rush through her body. A tingle deep within her started to grow. It began in the pit of her stomach and slowly spread up to her chest, making her heart pound faster. Then her arms and hands began to tingle as if they'd been asleep. The sensation intensified and spread to her legs. It felt like a thousand needles pricking her all over her body.

Then she felt her knees hitting against something hard, and she looked down.

*The floor! I can feel the floor!*

She felt soft fur rub against her forearms, followed by a wet lick.

She looked down to see Bear licking her arm. *She can feel me!*

"Mijita!"

Naomi looked up, and Welita's hands flew out and cupped her face. "I can see you! Mejita, I can see you!" She sobbed.

"Welita!" She threw herself into her arms. She didn't know how she was able to make herself appear in human form to Welita. She was never shown how to do that. It didn't matter. For now, she wanted to cherish the moment.

After a few minutes, Naomi pulled back, sniffling and brushing off tears with the back of her hand. She went to the corner of the room where there was a portable table covered in a cheap plastic yellow table cover, and took a chair. Placing it next to Welita, she sat down and scooped up Bear.

"I miss this." She laughed as Bear went wild licking her face.

Welita reached out and held Naomi's hand. "I've prayed to see you one last time. Thank you, Lord, for answering my prayers. I didn't think I would ever have a chance. After you left, I didn't see Rebecca anymore. I sensed her presence once in a while, but she never appeared to me again."

"Uh, Welita. I wasn't really sent here." She squirmed in her seat under Welita's scrutiny. "I'm supposed to be watching someone else. I'm really not supposed to be here."

"Naomi!" Welita took out a handkerchief from the pocket of her pale blue housedress and fanned herself. "You were not raised like that. We raised you to be a good girl."

"I know, Welita. But I just had to see you. Besides, Jeremy said it was okay."

She stopped fanning. "Who's Jeremy?"

"He's an archangel. He's here with me."

Welita looked around. "Right now?"

"Not *here* here. He's looking over the person I'm supposed to be watching over."

Welita gave her 'the look,' and she shrank back. It was a look that could put the fear of God in full-grown men.

Welita may have looked older and frailer, but that look of hers could still scare the crap out of anyone.

"He's doing your work for you?"

"Just for a while. It's a favor, really."

"And Lash? Where is he?"

Her heart lurched at the sound his name. She gazed down, studying Bear's fur as she brushed her hand over it. "He's still in Heaven."

"Look at me." Welita's voice was firm. "Tell me what happened."

Slowly, she lifted her eyes to meet Welita's. How could she tell her what happened? Welita would be devastated if she knew what Lash had done.

"I-I can't."

"You love him?"

"Yes, but it's more complicated than that."

"What's complicated about love?"

She sighed. She wanted so badly to tell her, to take the weight she was feeling off her chest.

"I can't explain, Welita. It's just...complicated."

"Yes, you can explain." She leaned over and cupped her cheek. "Don't be afraid."

Naomi felt Welita's strength from that simple touch as if she were passing it to her.

She placed Bear on the floor, and taking a deep breath she blurted, "I know how dad died."

Welita inhaled sharply. "He was hit by that senator woman... Jane Sutherland. She was driving drunk. We all know that."

"Do you remember when dad was little and was in the plane crash and the girl who survived the crash too?"

"How could I forget? I remember thinking that the angels were looking after God's children."

"Well, the little girl who survived was Jane Sutherland."

"Really?"

"And, well, she wasn't supposed to survive that accident." She stopped, unable to continue.

"Naomi, tell me." Welita reached over and placed a hand over hers. "Tell me."

She couldn't hold it in anymore. Tears ran down her face as the words rushed out in one breath. "It was Lash. Lash saved Jane. Oh Welita, he didn't know this would happen. I know he did it because he cares so much for people, I just know it. But, if he'd just done what he was supposed to do, dad would still be here, and, and..." She took a gulp of air. "...and maybe I would still be here, too. And we'd still be in Houston, and...and Chuy and Lalo wouldn't have lost their jobs, and there wouldn't be stupid bulldozers tearing down the neighborhood."

Welita held out her handkerchief, and Naomi took it, wiping her nose. "And I keep thinking about that over and over in my head: if only Lash hadn't saved her. And...and then I think I would've never met him. And maybe I wouldn't be as happy as I was when I was with him, but then I wouldn't be as miserable as I am now. Welita, I'm so confused."

Like she used to do when she was little, she threw herself at Welita and dropped her head into her lap, weeping. Bear licked her fingers, trying to comfort her, and that made her cry even harder.

Welita rubbed her back and softly crooned. Spanish rolled off her tongue as she sang the lyrics to Señora Santa Ana, a song she'd always sing to Naomi when she was a little girl and feeling sick. Slowly, Naomi began to feel calmer. Somehow, Welita always found a way to make her feel better, even now when she was an angel, the one who was supposed to help humans, not the other way around.

"Mejita, one of the hardest days in my life was having to bury my own son. It's something I wouldn't wish on my own enemies. It helped ease the pain knowing that Javier was with your mother. Rebecca told me that when he went to the other side, he was reunited with her. And when you left with Lash, that was also hard. But like your father, I knew that you were with Lash, that you had a love that was everlasting with him."

"You're not mad?"

"Mad at Lash? How can I be angry with the person who brings light to your eyes whenever you see him? Even now when you speak of him, you say his name with such love. How could I be mad at someone with such compassion in his heart that he dares to defy orders? You two are the same—a perfect match."

"Welita, I don't know what to do. I was so hurt when he told me. I felt betrayed, like he took something away from me. I mean, I know it wasn't intentional, and I think

I understand what he was thinking when he did it, but I can't help what I feel." She thought about the struggle she'd felt when she wanted to leave Megan and protect Chuy. It was the hardest thing she ever had to do.

"Let go of your anger and believe in him. Believe in your love. Lean on it. Love is strength."

"I don't know if I can. I don't even know if I can be a good angel," she said, her voice barely above a whisper. "Angels are supposed to be perfect. I'm not."

"Ay, Naomi, angels are not perfect. No one is. We are all made in the Lord's image, and He too feels anger, jealousy, so why not his angels? Why not you?"

"Angels are supposed to have faith. I don't know if I have that anymore. I almost messed up my first job by..." She hesitated, not wanting to tell her about Chuy almost dying. "Well, there was a courageous person who I thought was going to die in a fire, and I was supposed to watch over someone else, and I didn't want to."

"You do have faith. I know you do. You've always been stubborn, Mejita. Sometimes it works for you, and sometimes it works against you. Can't you see you're fighting against Lash's love because to accept it means to accept your place with the angels?" Welita cupped Naomi's face and stared intently into her eyes. "Your place is with them now. Surrender yourself to his love, and the rest will fall into place."

Naomi heard the sound of heels clacking down the hall, heading towards the room. Bear jumped off her lap and ran to the door, barking. "Someone's coming."

There was a soft rapping on the door. "Mrs. Duran. It's Jane Sutherland. May I please have a word with you?"

*Shit! Did Lucifer send her here?* Naomi listened carefully for any signs out of the ordinary.

"Don't let her in," she whispered furiously when Welita reached for her walker.

"Why not?"

"She's dangerous. She works with Lucifer."

Welita gasped and made the sign of the cross and muttered a quick prayer. "Are you sure?"

"Yes. Luke Prescott is Lucifer."

"Does she know?"

"I don't know."

"Then we must tell her."

"She won't believe you."

"You don't know that. There must be some good in her for Lash to see it and want to save her."

"That was a long time ago. The senator may have been innocent back then, but she's a powerful woman now. And may soon be the leader of the most powerful nation in the world. She and Lucifer together would be unstoppable." Naomi shuddered at the thought.

"Mrs. Duran?" There was another knock.

Welita turned to Naomi. "Both of you showing up here at the same time is too much of a coincidence for me to ignore. I need to see it through."

"Fine." Naomi sighed. "But I'm staying here until she leaves." She looked quickly around the tiny room. There was no place for her to hide. She couldn't let the senator see her. She wasn't sure if the senator knew about her death. More importantly, she didn't want any information going back to Lucifer.

Naomi closed her eyes and wondered if she would be able to change into her angel form. If she replicated what she'd done before, she should be able to change back—she hoped. "Okay, let her in."

# 15

Jane heard Anita Duran talking to someone through the closed door, and she wondered if someone was visiting her. She thought maybe her grandson, Chuy, was there with her, but when Anita opened the door, she was surprised to find her alone.

"Mrs. Duran, I'm sorry to bother you this late in the evening. I'll only take a few moments of your time."

When she stepped into the room, a small dog ran up to her. "What a precious dog," she said, reaching out to touch the dog.

It snapped at her.

"Oh!" She jerked her hand away.

"Bear! Don't be rude to our guest," Anita said. "Would you like something to drink, Senator?"

"Please allow me. I can get myself a glass of water."

Jane watched as Anita nodded and slowly maneuvered her walker as she made her way back to the sofa. Maybe this wasn't a good idea, digging up old wounds.

She grabbed a glass from a small open shelf in the corner of the room that served as a kitchen. Turning on the faucet, she made small talk. "It's pretty hot out there—almost as humid as it gets in Houston."

"Senator Sutherland, I don't mean to be rude, but you didn't come all this way from DC to talk about the weather."

Jane took a sip of water and then turned to face her. "Actually, I'm in town to make an important announcement."

"Your run for the presidency."

"Why, yes," Jane said, surprised.

"Don't look so surprised. I watch the news."

"I'm sorry. I didn't mean for it to come out that way."

"No apology needed. Please, have a seat." Anita motioned to the chair across from where she was sitting. "Why are you here?"

"I hope you don't take this the wrong way, Mrs. Duran, but I wanted to"—she gulped—"I wanted to ask you a question about your son."

The silence in the room was thick. Anita's brown eyes seemed to bore into her, and Jane felt beads of sweat collecting on her forehead. She wiped a palm on her skirt and slowly took a sip of water, hoping Anita would say something—anything to break the tension.

"Ask your question," Anita finally said.

Jane let out a breath. "Your son, Javier, was he ever in a plane accident?"

"Yes, he was in the Flight 1724 accident when he was a boy. You and he were the only survivors. I thought you knew."

She felt the blood drain from her face. "I-I-I was told that the Javier Duran I was with on the plane passed away years ago."

"You were misinformed, Senator. I'm surprised. I thought someone in your position would get accurate information."

"I got the information from a reliable source. Or at least, I thought so," Jane mumbled.

"Who would that be?"

"Luke Prescott's people." Jane lifted the glass of water to her lips.

"That's your problem right there. Mr. Prescott is Lucifer."

Jane spit the water out of her mouth, coughing. "Excuse me?"

"I said Luke Prescott is Lucifer, one of the fallen. A powerful dark angel that walks the Earth."

Something inside of Jane stirred when she looked into Anita's eyes, and for a moment, she actually believed her.

Jane pushed the thought from her mind. It was preposterous. There was no such thing as the devil, Lucifer, or whatever name people called evil spirits. She wondered if Anita had lost her mind. Maybe that was why she'd been put in this home. "That's a bit far-fetched, don't you think? I mean even if Luke lied to me, that wouldn't make him evil."

"He *is* evil. I know because my Naomi told me so."

"Naomi? The granddaughter who disappeared? When did she tell you this?"

"Just now."

"Is she here?" The poor woman was having hallucinations. She made a mental note to have her personal physician check in on Anita.

"She's sitting right next to me."

"She is?" She recalled Luke mentioning a good psychologist, Dr. Ryan Dantan. Maybe she should give him a call and ask for a consult. She could fly him in from Houston—at her own expense.

"You can't see her, and I can't either at this moment. But she appeared to me earlier. She told me she wouldn't leave until after you left."

"I see." Jane stood, walked to the kitchen, and placed the glass in the sink.

"Senator, even if you don't believe me about my granddaughter, it's not hard to see that what Luke Prescott is doing is harmful to us all."

"I'm not sure I understand what you mean."

"All of my neighbors have been talking about it. My grandson works for Prescott Oil, and he sees it too. Whatever that company is doing to the land is bad. What's it called?"

"Hydrofracturing."

"Yes, hydrofracturing. It's doing more harm than good. I even read that he plans to take it to other countries. What is happening here: the earthquakes, the bad water, will spread."

"I've heard this all before, Mrs. Duran. The media has a way of sensationalizing everything. I honestly believe that we can do good for many more people." She glanced over at a photo, noticing the dark handsome features of the young man she recognized as Chuy. "Your grandson has benefited from working with the company. He and many other families wouldn't have had a job if it wasn't for Prescott Oil."

Distress washed over Anita's face, and Jane felt horrible for what she had said.

"If it wasn't for me, my Chuy would never have taken the job. It pains me that I couldn't do anything to help him, and I ask for forgiveness every night for that."

"I'm sorry, Mrs. Duran. I didn't mean it that way."

Anita sighed and smoothed her face. "Javier told me what you did for him when he was on the plane. I know there is good in you. Can't you see that the person you're supporting, the one you call friend, is creating nothing but destruction to the country you love?"

"I don't see things the same way you do. Besides, that wouldn't make someone a devil."

She turned and headed to the door. She'd read the scientific reports and felt confident about hydrofracturing at the time. So why were Anita's words stirring something inside of her? Stirring fear that maybe she was right. "Mrs.

Duran, thank you for your time. Again, I'm so sorry to disturb you."

"Do you believe in God?"

Jane stopped abruptly, her hand on the doorknob. What kind of question was that? "Of course I do."

"Then why can't you believe that what I've said is true?"

"Well, because...because..." Jane turned to face Anita, and she was at a loss for words. Thoughts flashed through her mind: what she'd overheard Luke telling Sal, Luke attempting to sway her vote, and the serious expression on Anita's face.

Suddenly, she felt feverish, and a heavy feeling pressed on her chest. She couldn't breathe. She had to get out. Now. "Good-bye Mrs. Duran."

She ran down the hall and out of the building. Her heart slammed against her chest a hundred miles a minute as she plucked a set of car keys from out of her purse. She needed to leave, to get far away from there. Far away from the memories that fluttered through her mind: the presence of someone near her during the plane crash, protecting her; the same presence protecting her during the auto accident; Luke rising to the top of the corporate world in unprecedented speed, never aging, always the same. If she believed in God, how could she not believe in evil?

No. It wasn't possible. It couldn't be possible. Luke was not Lucifer. He wasn't the devil.

Her hands shook, and the keys slipped out of her hand, falling onto the pavement. When she bent down to pick them up, a cold chill swept through her. She could feel someone watching her every move.

She glanced up and froze when she saw a pair of crocodile boots.

She blinked, and they were gone.

After the senator left, Naomi reluctantly gave Welita a kiss good-bye, promising to watch over her and Chuy whenever she could. When she arrived back in Emma's hospital room, Megan was asleep and Jeremy was nowhere to be found.

Looking out the window, she saw him in a grove of trees across the hospital parking lot, sitting on one of the tree branches. He must've seen her because he waved and gestured for her to join him.

After crossing the lot, Naomi glided through a field of wildflowers that were dispersed in small patches near the trees. Craning her neck, she watched Jeremy swing his legs like a little boy. He wore a silly grin that lit up his face. He almost looked like the Jeremy she'd first met in New Mexico.

He jumped out of the tree and gracefully landed in front of her. For the first time, she really looked at him and realized that he looked different from when they had first met.

Gone were his usual black suit and crisp white shirt. He wore a simple of pair of jeans that hugged his hips. A soft-looking black leather jacket was thrown over a simple white cotton T-shirt.

She eyed him carefully. It was something she could imagine Lash wearing.

"Why don't you wear your suits anymore?"

His smile froze, and after a moment, he gave a forced laugh. "I gotta keep up with the latest trends. Besides, I had a feeling this assignment would require more wash-n-wear clothing."

His eyes locked with hers briefly before he quickly diverted them. He walked a few steps away from her and plopped himself on the grass. "So guess what Chuy and Lalo are up to."

She sank down beside him, crossing her legs Indian style. "I'm almost afraid to ask."

"They were able to get some evidence that Prescott Oil is illegally dumping the chemicals they're using. Lalo somehow even managed to get proof that they're not lining the wells according to Federal regulations. I don't know how he got it, but he did. Chuy is going to sneak Megan into the press conference. She's going to try to make a scene to attract media attention and then give them the evidence."

She shook her head. "I hope it works. It didn't work for me."

He gave her a questioning look.

"Long story." She sighed, remembering how she'd crashed the senator's fundraising banquet only to be immediately tossed out. "I guess that means I'll be there too."

"Yeah, the both of us."

"Don't you need to stay with Emma?"

He cursed under his breath and turned his head away from her.

She studied his profile, watching his square jaw tense. "What's wrong?"

"Nothing. So, how did it go?"

Great. He was changing the subject. It was no use pressing him to tell her.

"She's not the same," she said. "It was hard seeing her like that."

"Is she okay?"

"Yeah, I guess. I mean, she seems to be doing well, but she looked so fragile. The year has really taken a toll on her. And..."

She hesitated to tell him what she had done, appearing to Welita. Would he get mad?

"And what?" he prodded with sapphire eyes that glowed with openness. He was on her side. She could trust him.

"And she saw me."

He grinned, dimples flashing. "Did she freak?"

She laughed. "Of course not. She already knew I was there. My grandmother has always believed in angels. Didn't Lash tell you that your mother was her guardian angel?"

There was a tense silence. Hurt passed over his face, and she bit down on her lip. How could she forget that Lash was barely on speaking terms with him?

"I'm sorry. I forgot about you and...well, what about Raphael? Didn't he tell you about Rebecca and my grandmother?"

"I haven't been talking that much to Raphael lately, either. I had to leave soon after you were reunited with Lash. I was sent on assignment, remember? Raphael mentioned it."

"Oh, right. Why were you sent on a job so soon? I thought Gabrielle would cut you some slack. She likes *you.*"

He studied her face for a moment, and she felt that pull again, as if he was silently urging her to him. After a moment, he let out a breath and looked away. "I wasn't really on an assignment. I had some...things I had to do."

"Oh. I didn't mean to pry."

He groaned and fell back into the grass, gazing at the stars in the cloudless sky. "It's not easy being the angel of death."

She furrowed her brow, wondering what he was talking about. "I can imagine."

When he turned his head toward her, long spears of grass brushed against his flawless face. "I wasn't happy being a seraph. I wanted to be an archangel. I even tried to convince Lash to be one too. He didn't want it. I thought he was holding himself back and being his rebellious self.

Now I know it was because being an archangel would've stifled him, taken the best out of him."

She knew exactly what he meant. She felt the burden of being an archangel, and she hadn't even completed her training yet. *Oh, Lash. Welita is right—we are a perfect match.*

He chuckled as he continued to reminisce. "You should've seen the things he did to rile up Gabrielle. I miss him."

She felt an ache in her chest. She missed Lash too. What she wouldn't do to have him there at this moment. She desperately wanted to see him and tell him she was sorry: sorry for staying mad at him, for hurting him, and that she understood now why he'd done what he did.

"There's one thing about being the archangel of death that amazes me though."

"What's that?"

"People can be so strong in the face of death." He sat up, bracing himself on his elbows. "Almost everyone I've had to take over to the other side finds a way to put themselves at peace with it. They ask forgiveness from loved ones or mutter a prayer. But the ones that amaze me the most are those who take danger head on, knowing they'll more than likely die, and yet they face that danger anyway. And the psalm they mutter. It's so beautiful."

She thought back to her catechism classes, remembering that a psalm is like a song or prayer. There were so many. "Which one?"

"You know the one that starts off with 'Yea, though I walk through the valley of the shadow of death'?"

"Yeah. You like that one?"

He nodded. "There's something about it when a person mutters it under his breath, you can feel a sense of peace. Like they're resolved to face their death. Sometimes, I wonder if I would be able to do something like that."

"What do you mean? Face your own death?"

"I don't know if I'm strong enough to do it." He barked a laugh. "Imagine that. The angel of death afraid of dying."

"Why would you even think it?" Her mind flashed to Uri and Rachel.

He pulled himself up and walked a few feet away from her. "Because, I guess, deep inside, I know I'm a coward."

"No, you're not." She went to him and turned him around to face her. "You and Lash are the bravest people I know. You had to make sure I got to the top of Shiprock. And you had to do it without telling your best friend. I know he's still mad at you, but he'll come around. And you had to know that he'd get mad even though you were doing what was best for him."

Jeremy dropped his head. "You think too much of me. I didn't know you were going to join us. I was just doing my duty."

"I wasn't talking about me. You knew that he'd go back home after you...uh, after your job was done."

"Say it, Naomi. After I killed you."

"Jeremy, look at me." Her hand reached out to him, and when it touched his strong jaw, his breath hitched. He tried to pull away from her, but she firmly lifted his head to make his eyes meet hers.

"Naomi, please don't." His voice was raw.

"Don't what? Don't tell you 'You're a wonderful brother'? Don't tell you 'You've been a great friend to me'?"

"If you knew what I was feeling, you wouldn't be saying those things."

"I know you may be…confused about your feelings for me, but—"

"I'm not confused," he said, his sapphire eyes gazed deeply into hers.

"Jeremy. You may think that right now, but with time, as you get to know me, you'll see things…you'll see us more clearly. There's one thing I know for certain." She placed a hand on his chest. "This heart loves his family deeply and will do anything for them."

His eyes smoldered at her touch, and she swallowed at their intensity. He reached out, and his fingers ghosted over her face as if memorizing every single inch. When they reached her lips, she gasped as his thumb gently stroked her bottom lip. Slowly, he leaned in toward her, lips parting. She was about to pull away from him when something crashed into his body, sending him twenty feet into the air.

A blur whirled past her, straight to where Jeremy lay groaning. She was about to run to him when the shadow stopped and turned to face her.

*Lash!*

# 16

Naomi's heart skipped a beat at the glorious sight of Lash. His hazel eyes blazed with fury as he stared down at Jeremy. His fist clenched tightly against his side, muscles straining, tensing, ready to fight. The sides of his jaw jutted out, and he gritted his teeth, emphasizing his handsome chiseled face.

"Lash," she breathed.

He turned, and his face softened when his eyes met hers. "Naomi. I'm sorry about...everything."

She heard a groan, and her eyes darted to Jeremy as he lifted himself from the ground. Whirling, Lash took a threatening step towards him.

Naomi rushed to Lash and grasped his arm. "Don't. He's your brother."

Hurt flashed across his eyes as he studied her face. "You"—he swallowed thickly—"care for him?"

"Of course I do."

He sucked in a breath as if he'd been punched.

"He's my brother too," she explained. "At least, he will be soon."

He blinked and looked at her as if he couldn't believe what she was saying. "You still want to be bound to me? You forgive me?"

"Yes! Yes!"

Before she could say another word, fevered lips pressed down on hers with such passion, she felt like she would float away at any minute. Tears streamed down her face, thinking of how stupid she'd been to hurt him the way she did. She kissed him back deeply. Her arms clung to his neck as she drowned herself in his kiss. This was where she belonged, in his arms.

"Oh Lash, I love you," she said in between kisses. "I have always loved you. I'm so sorry I left like I did."

"Naomi, I was so scared. I thought you'd stop loving me."

"Never...no matter what."

He paused and pulled back. Gazing at her tenderly, he brushed the tears from her cheeks. "Why are you crying?"

"Because I'm so happy."

He chuckled and placed his forehead on hers. "I'm happy too."

There was a sudden movement coming from behind Lash that caught her eye. Her heart flew to her throat at the sight of Jeremy's face. Red with fury, it grew closer as he charged at them.

"Lash, look out!"

Before he could turn, a pair of arms lifted him off the ground. She screamed as iron claws also cut into her shoulders and jerked her up.

Jeremy dove and crashed into whatever it was that had grabbed her. The entity let out a grunt and released her, sending her slamming to the ground.

As she scrambled to get on her feet, Jeremy crouched in front of her. "Get behind me!"

"Impressive, Jeremiel. I see domestic bliss hasn't softened you. You managed to put down one of my best fighters."

Her heart fell to the pit of her stomach at the sound of the familiar voice. A hulking shadow moved out from behind the trees, and she clutched Jeremy's arm when she saw who it was.

"You're not touching her, Saleos," Jeremy growled as the dark angel he'd taken down got up and took his place beside Sal.

"Oh, I'm not interested in touching her...yet." Sal smirked, waving over to someone behind him. A second dark angel emerged from the shadows, an exact replica of the one who had attacked Naomi. They both had the same beady black eyes and shaved heads. They looked exactly like the demons in a child's nightmare.

The dark angel dragged something behind him, pulling it from the shadow. He let out a frustrated roar as he jerked forward, throwing Lash in front of him. A massive arm quickly wrapped around Lash's throat, and another clinched him by the waist.

"No!" Naomi screamed as she charged toward them. "Let him go!"

"Don't." Jeremy grabbed her arm, pulling her back.

"I see you're the one who wants to do the touching, Jeremiel," Sal said. "You've been at it for quite some time. How long was it, ten, fifteen minutes?"

Lash growled at his words and attempted to lunge after Sal. When he managed to get one arm loose, the dark angel's twin grabbed it and twisted it behind his back. Lash howled in pain.

"Please, don't hurt him," Naomi sobbed. "Let him go. I'll go with you."

"Aw, so sweet. She wants to sacrifice herself for you, Lahash. It must be *love*." Sal sneered the word. "I wonder if she would still be willing to after spending a night with Jeremiel. Hmm?"

Lash turned red and kicked his feet up, struggling against the dark angel's grip. The dark angel yanked him back, laughing.

"Don't listen to him, Lash," Jeremy pleaded.

Lash stopped struggling and glared at Jeremy. "I saw you. I know what you were doing. You lied to me!"

"It's not like that," Jeremy said. "She loves you."

"And you love her! Admit it!" he spat.

"Tell him, Jeremy," Naomi said, touching his arm. "Tell him you're just confused. It's not what he thinks."

Sapphire eyes looked down at her, and raw emotion filled his handsome face.

"I can't," he croaked.

"No," she whispered. She didn't want it to be this way. Lash needed his big brother. "Please...just tell him."

Jeremy bowed his head and turned. It was as if he couldn't bear to face Lash. "You're right. I love her."

Lash let out a stream of curses. His fury was so intense, it took both evil twins to hold him down.

A loud clapping pierced the night air as Sal took a step toward Jeremy. "Well played, my friend. You can't remember the past, and yet centuries later, you've still managed to keep Naomi by your side. You even got her assigned to work with you."

"He's lying. I never wanted to hurt you," Jeremy said to Lash before turning to Sal. "And I am *not* your friend."

"Oh, I'm hurt," Sal said. "Really, I am. Well, this family drama has been entertaining, but I fear we must leave now. Say your good-byes, Lahash."

The evil twins started to drag Lash away.

"No! Not him!" It didn't make any sense. She was the one they were after. They'd bought out her entire neighborhood and gotten Welita and Chuy to leave and be placed under Lucifer's watchful eye. They were here for her. "Take me. You're here for me."

Jeremy pulled her to his chest, restraining her. The dark twins ignored her pleas as they let out their black wings, ready to take flight.

*They can't be leaving. They can't.* Naomi struggled against Jeremy's strong grip, trying to get to the man she loved.

"Lash, I love you!"

"Naomi, stop," Lash said with an eerie calm.

Her eyes locked with his, and a cold swept through her at the expression on his face. It was the same way he'd looked at her when she was dying. It was as if he was saying good-bye to her. "You'll always be in my heart," he whispered.

He squeezed his eyes shut and muttered something to himself. He then took a deep breath, as if he'd made a decision. Opening his eyes, he turned to Jeremy, looking at him intently.

"Jeremy, listen to me," he said in a low rumble. "I'm depending on your love for her. Do *not* let Sal or Lucifer get their hands on her. Promise me."

"You have my word. I'll watch over her as I would a sister."

With those words, the dark angels flapped their wings, sending a strong gust through the trees, and flew away up into the sky. In an instant, they disappeared.

Lash was gone.

"No!" Naomi shrieked. She elbowed Jeremy hard in his stomach, making him drop to his knees, groaning. Flicking out her wings, she instantly went after them.

*Where are they? Whcrc did they go?* Tears streamed down her face as she circled the night sky. They were nowhere in sight. She was about to climb higher when

Jeremy tackled her and they fell, slamming onto the ground.

"Let go of me." She clawed and punched at him. "I need to go after them. Let. Me. Go!"

She punched him in the face with a loud crack.

"She *is* a wild one." Sal cackled in the background.

She dove at Sal, but before she reached him, Jeremy threw himself on top of her. "Damn it, Jeremy!"

He helped her to her feet and stood behind her, his strong arms holding her in a tight grip. "I'm not letting you place yourself in danger."

Ignoring Jeremy, she growled at Sal. "Take me, Asshole! You know Lucifer wants me. I'll give you anything you want."

Sal arched an eyebrow. "Anything?"

She froze. An icy chill went through her as Sal's eyes traveled up and down her body.

She gulped. "Yes, anything."

"I won't let you," Jeremy hissed. "She's not for the taking, Saleos."

He smirked. "You offer is...interesting, but I'm afraid I can't take it at this time...although I think you would've enjoyed yourself."

With a loud cracking sound, he spread his wings out to their full length and elevated up into the sky. Circling them, he said, "After all, I have body parts that are more impressive than the size of my wings."

"Wait! Lucifer wants *me*. You know he does."

Sal threw his head back and laughed. "He never wanted you. You were just bait."

When Sal disappeared, Naomi's legs gave out and she sank to the ground. She was so confused. While she was human, she'd been running to get away from Lucifer. Sal had hunted her down. He'd shot at her...twice! It even got Deborah and Nathan killed. Why had they put so much effort into trying to kill her, get rid of her, and now changed their minds?

"I don't understand. Why Lash? What are they going to do to him?"

Jeremy stood off alone to the side, his face unreadable, staring off in the direction the dark angels had gone with Lash.

"Jeremy?"

He shook his head as if clearing it. "I'm sorry. What were you saying?"

"Why are they after Lash?"

"I don't know."

She sighed. "If I can't trade myself for him, then we'll just have to get him back by force."

She stood up with a determined look on her face. "Okay, so we need to go back and let the others know what happened. We can come up with a plan to save him."

She began to pace. "Now, how can we find him? I know. I'll ask Raphael. Maybe he'll know where they took him." She turned to Jeremy. "Come on, let's go."

"We can't go."

"Why?"

Jeremy looked in the direction of the hospital. "We have jobs to do."

She balked. "You've got to be kidding me. Are you telling me that I have to stay here and look over Megan?"

"Yes. It's your duty."

She looked back at the hospital, at the window to the room where Emma lay struggling for her life. Her job was to look over Megan. If she left, would that mean something would happen to Megan, leaving Emma all alone?

"Emma's father will be here soon. And, I'm sure Megan will be okay. Besides, you let me go see Welita." She bent her knees, ready to take flight.

"That was before." Jeremy grabbed her arm.

"Before what?"

"Before I knew what Megan and Chuy have planned for the morning."

She rolled her eyes. "That? Crashing in on a press conference? The most that will happen is they'll sic the cops on her. Maybe get her charged with a misdemeanor. It's nothing."

"No, Naomi. You stay here. I'll go."

He looked nervously back at the hospital.

"Why won't you let me go? It's just Megan."

A look of pain crossed Jeremy's face. "It's more than that."

"What is it? What are you not telling me?"

"I wasn't here for Emma."

Naomi let out a rush of air. "She's going to live." She was so relieved. Why was he telling her this now?

"Yes, I believe so."

"That's why you helped her?"

He nodded.

"So you were here for Megan's aunt."

"I wasn't here for her, either."

Dread washed over her, and she fought against the voices in the back of her head that told her the answer.

"Who?" her voice was barely above a whisper.

"Chuy."

# 17

The chamber was exactly the way Rachel had described it. A lake of lava surrounded Lash, licking his feet, blackening the tips of his toes.

A narrow path lined with fiery liquid and barely a foot wide led straight to where he hung chained against the wall. That was the only way to him other than flying...if an angel was able to get into this nightmare of a place.

When Sal and the evil twins brought him in, even they were not immune to the powers of the Lake of Fire. The pit of Hell sucked the life source out of anyone who entered it.

Sal had stood back while the twins struggled to fly over the lake. Once they crossed, they had stripped Lash of his clothes and chained him to the wall. It was like Rachel had said. In the pit of Hell, even the strongest angel's powers were diminished, even those of the fallen.

The twins had barely made it back to land after they chained him. Sal had thrown him one last look of disgust and then they left him alone.

Lash took a deep breath, gathered his strength, and tried for the hundredth time to break free from the heavy chains strapped to his chest and waist. As he strained, the ropes of red-hot steel pressed against his naked body, scorching him. He screamed in agony, the sound echoing through the vast tunnels surrounding the Lake of Fire.

His head lay limp on his chest, lolling back and forth. The fiery heat of the lava and the burning steel that was cinched to him like a snake of death sapped every ounce of his strength. Minutes passed feeling like hours as the chains continued to burn his skin. He tried not to move, but even that didn't work because all the while the walls cracked, allowing lava to ooze through the fissures onto his back and wings.

In between the haze of pain, he thought of Uri. Was this what it had been like for him? Skin charring right before his eyes with each passing minute. The inescapable pain made worse with the slightest movement. But what was worse, much worse, was the fear that Naomi would come after him and see him like this, the way Rachel had when she went after Uri.

He prayed that Jeremy would keep his word and watch over her. Why wouldn't he? Jeremy would finally have what he'd wanted since even before he had memories of her. With him gone, Jeremy had Naomi for himself.

The image of Jeremy holding Naomi was seared into his mind, and he winced at the excruciating pain in his chest, not from the chains but from Naomi loving someone else. As much as it pained him, at least he knew that she would be loved the way she should be and not by some screw-up like himself.

He let out a staggered breath. It was for the best. For some reason, Lucifer wanted him dead. Maybe Lucifer was using him to antagonize Michael. Or maybe he thought he would lure the other angels to the lake to save him. Lucifer was an idiot if he thought it'd work. No one would come for him. He wasn't important enough. It wasn't like he was Gabrielle or even Uri. He was just a lowly seraph.

The only one who would care was Naomi. And as long as Jeremy kept his word, she was safe and would never set foot in here. He'd rather die than have her in harm's way.

"Naomi," he moaned, needing to say her name. It was his only comfort. He was dying, and he knew it.

He closed his eyes and concentrated on the image of her face, the only thing that could keep him sane.

He thought of the way she'd looked at him the last time they were together. Soft lips like rose petals kissing him gently. Lips that brushed his ear when whispering words of love. Lips that curled into a smile whenever he entered the room.

He remembered holding her in his arms when he first told her that he was an angel. The way her body molded perfectly into his. The way her fingers gently stroked his jaw and how she reached out to kiss him. And then the torment of him pulling away from her, afraid to kiss her because once he did, he wouldn't be able to let her go. And the blissful moment when he finally did kiss those lips and discovered that he had found home in her arms. She was his destiny, his soul mate.

Footsteps echoed in the corridor, and for a moment, hope leaped into his chest.

"Ah, Lahash. You are a sight."

Lash slowly lifted his head, wincing at the movement. "Lucifer."

"Please, don't move on my account. It's a great hardship for me to see you in such...discomfort," Lucifer said. "Saleos, excellent work. Did I not tell you, 'Where the girl is, the boy will follow'?"

"That you did. Although I'm still not convinced that your plan will work," Sal replied.

"Ah, ye of little faith. Let's see about that, shall we?"

"What..." Lash gasped as a wave of lava splashed against the wall, sending droplets of searing heat onto his feet. "What plan?"

Lucifer sauntered around the edge of the lava as he spoke. "I have a proposition for you, my son. It's one I've made to you before, remember?"

A memory of Naomi lying in his arms on the top of Shiprock flashed through his mind.

*I can save her. All you have to do is ask.* The words Lucifer had said at Shiprock echoed in his mind.

"I didn't go with you then, and I won't now. And don't even bother going after her. She's already an archangel in training. The others will look after her until she grows in strength."

Lucifer stopped and looked at Lash, his lips curling into a smile that made Lash's hair stand on end. "Ah, but it is not Naomi I seek. It is you."

"That's a lie, and you know it. You had Sal hunt her down. There's no reason why you would want me."

"Come now, my son. Surely, by this time, you know why."

"Stop it! Stop calling me that!" Lash tugged on the chain and screeched in pain as it singed his skin like a branding iron.

"Calm yourself, Lahash. You'll only do yourself more harm by struggling. Perhaps now is the time for me to tell you a story about Raphael, your mother"—his lips curled into a wicked smile—"and me."

"I don't want to hear it," he moaned.

"How do the humans like to start their stories? Ah, yes…once upon a time there were two devilishly handsome, excuse the pun, archangels. They were the best of friends—not unlike you and Jeremiel."

Sal laughed. "If you can still call them that."

"No interruptions, Saleos. You know the story. Now it's Lahash's turn to hear it. Now where was I? Ah, yes…the best friends decided to journey to Earth for a spell. You see, the golden-haired angel fell in love with a woman on Earth, and his friend, well, let's just say he didn't want to limit himself to just one woman. Now, the golden angel lived in marital bliss with the woman, and they had a son, a son who looked just like him, a perfect replica. One day, the golden angel was away with his perfect son...he was so proud of his progeny, wasn't he Saleos?"

Sal nodded. "He was a god among men."

"Yes, he was, but I digress. Well, the hazel-eyed woman was a sight to behold. And the devilishly handsome archangel had lain with most of the beautiful women in the land, all except for one."

"No," Lash groaned. "I won't listen to your lies."

"Please, no interruptions. I haven't gotten to the best part yet," Lucifer said sweetly. "Oh, but you look in such pain. I'll get to the point. Nine months later, the lovely woman gave birth to a dark-haired son. The boy was different from his older brother, always questioning, doing his own will—the complete opposite of his brother and very much like his father. Can you guess who he is?"

"Lies. Lies. It's all a lie," Lash growled.

"Every word I've uttered, every vision I've shown you; they all are true." Lucifer's voice dropped to a low pitch. "And deep inside yourself, you know it."

Lash snarled and threw himself forward, desperate to get loose and strangle Lucifer. He gasped as the chains around his waist pressed against him, searing deep into him. His head fell to his chest as he struggled to breathe. "Raphael...Raphael is my father."

There was a rumble deep in Lucifer's chest. "Look at me, Lahash!"

Lash squeezed his eyes shut, refusing to listen to Lucifer's demands. He thought of Raphael and the words he had said to him in the courtyard not so long ago. "I've always been a father to you," he had said.

*I've always been a father to you.*

*I've always been a father to you.*

*A father.*

*A father.*

*My father.*

He held onto those words and repeated them in his mind like a mantra, refusing to listen to Lucifer's obvious deception.

He heard the sound of bubbling liquid, and a sudden gust of heat slammed into his body. Then searing liquid splattered onto his chest, and he wailed in agony.

Against his will, he felt his head being lifted and his eyes being drawn open. Once they were open, he saw Lucifer's hand up, manipulating him and the lava to do his will.

"Look at me and see the truth that is set before your eyes, Lahash. It is Raphael who has lied to you. He is not your father."

The cave grew still. The only sound was the crunching of volcanic rock as Lucifer took a step forward to the edge of the lake.

"I am."

Crushing waves of white noise filled Lash's ears, beating, pounding Lucifer's words into his mind.

*I am.*

*I am.*

*I am!*

Lash jerked his head to the side. *No! I won't believe!*

"Look at me, Lahash!"

Again his head was pulled in Lucifer's direction, and what he so desperately wanted to deny was standing right in front of him. He took in Lucifer's tall, lithe body, his dark wavy hair. A wave of cold smashed into his heart, shattering it into a million pieces. He closed his eyes in despair.

*It's true.* He moaned. That's why Raphael loved Jeremy. Jeremy was Raphael's true son, and he...he was a bastard.

"Ah, I see you have accepted your fate. You've never really fit in with Raphael and his family, heavenly or earthly. I regret that I did not take you in sooner, but I was young then, and my sole focus was to build my empire. By the time I was ready for you to join me, you were gone." He clapped his hands together and smiled. "Well, that's all in the past. Now we can start over. And with Naomi and you in our little family, we can defeat anyone who decides to challenge us as I move toward my total domination of Earth."

Lash's eyes flashed open. "I told you, she'll never join you, and neither will I," he seethed. "I don't care who you are. You can kill me, and still, Michael and the others will defeat you."

Lucifer laughed. "I do not fear Michael's army. His belief in the free will of man, or shall I say men and women, is his downfall. Oh, I'm very secure, and my association with Senator Jane Sutherland guarantees it. It is she who will lead us to the victory I seek."

"What are you talking about?"

"Lahash, I'm shocked. Surely, a seraph would have taken the time to learn human spiritual writings. Even Saleos here knows the prophecy. Tell him, Saleos."

"It is foretold that 'a woman, known as the whore of Babylon sitting on a scarlet beast, will make herself drunk with the blood of saints and will be the leader among leaders on Earth.' Anything else I need to teach him?" Saleos scowled.

"No, I'll take the liberty of telling him the good part," Lucifer said. "It is written that 'the beast'"—he grinned, tapping his broad chest—"'will hate the whore and will burn her with fire.' Hate is a strong word. Maybe not hate, but I do admit she's turning out to be a handful lately."

*What have I done?* Lash felt the blood drain from his face. All those years ago when he was on that plane, he had thought he was saving two children, instead of just the one he was assigned to. He thought he was saving a kind-hearted little girl, and now she turned out to be what humans considered the antichrist? Was this all his fault?

No, he had to believe that Michael would've had someone else go after her if they thought she was a threat. "That'll never happen. Michael will stop you both."

"Ah, but it has already begun. Although I will miss my dear sweet Jane once she has served her use." He looked intently at Lash. "My son, there is no need for *you* to have her fate. I ask you one last time. Will you join us?"

Lash glared at him. "No."

Lucifer's lips tightened into a thin line, and his eyes narrowed. "So, be it. Saleos, head out to the press conference in Gardenville. No one is to touch our precious Jane. Hear me?"

Sal nodded.

"You two," he snapped at the pair of dark angels. They went to him quickly and bowed. "Bring Naomi here. Alone. Have your way with her, then kill her."

Two pairs of black eyes turned to Lash, giving him an evil smirk.

"No!" Lash roared as he jerked on his chains. "Don't you touch her!"

Lucifer turned to him, his eyes cold. "Make sure he is kept alive long enough to see it."

# 18

Naomi stood at the entrance to the hospital room, watching Chuy as he slept. His large body was sprawled over the chair in the corner. On the other side of the room, Megan slept on the edge of Emma's bed, clutching her tiny hand. The only sounds in the room were the beeps and whirls of the machines and Chuy's soft snoring.

When she returned to the room, she had found Chuy and Megan planning how they would turn the media's attention to the damage Prescott Oil was doing to Gardenville and other small towns in Texas. Chuy had told her that Lalo was close to getting all the information they needed and would give it to them at the press conference, which was to be held in an open field just outside of Prescott Oil's business offices. Megan had made one final call to Emma's father, making sure that he would be there by morning to watch over her. It seemed everything was set and all they had to do was wait for morning.

The sun peeped out of the horizon, turning the sky into a haze of pink and purple. Naomi glanced at the clock and frowned. Jeremy wasn't back yet, and in only a few more hours, Chuy and Megan would be leaving to the location where Senator Sutherland was making her presidential announcement.

Jeremy had been gone for what seemed like a long time. She warred with the thought of going after him. But then she took one look at Chuy—long curly eyelashes fanning his brown face, his mouth slightly open as he slept, looking like a helpless little boy rather than a man—and she couldn't take the chance of leaving him. He was in danger. Jeremy's voice echoed in her mind. He was there for Chuy.

He wouldn't tell her what he meant by saying that. Of course he wouldn't. Even though he had admitted to being in love with her, he still wouldn't break the code of silence when it came to their assignments.

She leaned against the doorframe, wondering what Lash would've done. There was no doubt in her mind that he would've told her, even if it meant getting in trouble for it. To Lash, the people he looked over were more than assignments. He cared deeply for them. It wasn't that Jeremy didn't care. It was just that his loyalties were in a different place.

At the thought of Lash, her hands shook and her heart pounded. She quickly pushed the thought of him to the back of her mind. She'd go crazy if she didn't. She felt her nails dig into her palms as she clenched her hands into fists. It was taking every ounce of strength to wait for Jeremy. Only Chuy's safety was keeping her there.

Chuy stirred in his seat, and the sleeve of his T-shirt rolled up, revealing his tattoo. She wished she had been there to see the look on Welita's face when she found out about it. She could see her now, chasing him around the house with broom in hand, threatening to smack sense into him. Chuy probably would've pretended he was afraid and apologized profusely to her, promising to never do it again. Although Naomi knew he would've been planning on his next one even as he said it.

She sighed. Chuy was too young, too full of life to die, and Welita needed him. Maybe she could warn him, somehow. Even if she risked appearing to him like she had with Welita, what would she tell him: "Be careful and don't die anytime soon"? "Lash's brother is the archangel of death, and he's waiting around for something to happen to you, so don't die"?

She shook her head. She didn't want this kind of life. She didn't want to have to choose between saving Lash or saving Chuy. She hated being pulled in different directions. It felt like she was being torn in two. And there was nothing she could do to stop it.

Chuy shifted in the chair again, and a cell phone fell out of his lap. She glanced at him, seeing if the sound would wake him, but he continued to sleep.

There was only one person who could understand her. And she desperately wanted an answer.

She looked around the corridor, and seeing no one, she glided to Chuy. Standing over him, she willed herself to change into her human form.

Without making a sound, she picked up the phone and stepped out of the room into the hallway.

With a swipe and a few taps, she found Welita's number. She probably shouldn't be calling her. She had already crossed the line by visiting her, but she needed her.

"Que paso? What's wrong, Chuy? You're never up this early."

Naomi swallowed thickly at the sound of Welita's voice.

"Chuy?" There was a pause. "Naomi."

"Welita," she whispered, holding tightly to the phone. "I'm so sorry. I had to hear your voice one more time."

"What's wrong, Mejita?"

"I know something that I'm not supposed to know, and I want to do something about it. I want to tell that person, but I shouldn't, and I still want to...but...but what if the... thing is supposed to happen?"

"I haven't had my coffee yet. You're not making sense."

She closed her eyes and took a deep breath. "I think someone is going to die soon."

"Who?"

"It's... It's..." She couldn't lay that kind of burden on her. "I can't tell you."

Naomi heard Welita's breath hitch, followed by a muttered prayer. She didn't have to tell her. It was as if

Welita knew just by the sound of her voice. "Are you sure this person's life will end soon?"

"Yes. What do I do?"

There was silence at the end of the line. And then her voice came out soft yet firm. "You let God's plan unfold."

"But, Welita. I can do something about it. I'm an angel. Why shouldn't I help? I can't just stand by and watch him die."

"Ay, Mejita. We all die. Even if you were still here with us, someday you would've had to watch me die, bury me, and mourn for me."

She closed her eyes, and a single tear slid down her cheek. It was a cruel angel's fate to have all these powers and still not be able to stop the heartache of watching her loved ones die. "Why? Why is this so hard?"

"De la espina y el dolor nace la flor," Welita said gently.

"From the thorn and the pain a flower is born," Naomi repeated the Spanish proverb. It was Welita's favorite.

"You have hardship now, but in the end, I know that something wonderful will come of it. Not only for you, but for all of us."

There was so much more she wished she could tell Welita and ask for her wisdom on it all: how to show love for Jeremy without having him confuse it for something more than sisterly love; and Lash, my God, she wanted to go after him so badly.

As if hearing her thoughts, Welita asked, "What has Lash told you about this?"

She couldn't do it. She couldn't even say his name without her heart breaking. She was barely keeping herself together as it was. "Welita, I have to go. Just know that I love you...*we* love you."

Deep inside, she had already known the answer. All she could do now was rely on faith and hope. Faith that she had the strength to carry on watching over Megan and Chuy, and hope that Jeremy would return soon with an army of angels to save Lash.

And with that, she clicked off the phone.

# 19

It was a glorious morning with not a cloud in the sky, and all Jane could think about was how she wished it would rain. She fingered the material of her cream pantsuit nervously as she sat hidden behind the dark-tinted windows of the SUV, watching the mass of media assemble on the open field. Why had she agreed to do the announcement out in the open like this?

She eyed the Prescott Oil office building, which sat a couple of hundred yards away from the make-shift stage that had been slapped together overnight, compliments of the company's employees. A giant U.S. flag hung on the front, almost covering an entire wall of the three-story building. It was an impressive sight.

A few employees, dressed in blue coveralls with the Prescott Oil emblem emblazed on the right side of their chests, walked around the stage, doing last minute checks. On the lectern, there was the familiar cluster of microphones from news stations around the country. Behind the stage was a large sign with her smiling face and the words, *Sutherland for President*.

There was a steady trickle of people lining up in front of the stage. It was easy to tell the hard-core American Federation party supporters from the Prescott Oil employees who had been given the day off—only if they attended the rally. Members of the AF headed straight to Luke, giving him their congratulations on a good start to the campaign. Members of the community were directed to stand in the front row facing the stage where they were sure to be picked up by the cameras, obviously something Luke and his advisors orchestrated.

A pretty blonde woman wearing a pale yellow summer dress caught her eye. She was talking to one of the stage workers, a heavy-set man, his face partially hidden beneath a blue cap that matched his work uniform.

Jane peered through the window at the object the blonde woman had in her hands. Others in the audience were also waving something.

*Oh, my God. They have fans with my face on them.* She rolled her eyes, not knowing whether to admire Luke's marketing genius or to be embarrassed at watching her smiling face being waved about by dozens of people.

As much as she hated the idea of seeing her smiling face flapping at her when she was on stage, she wished she could have one. It was not even eight o'clock in the morning, and she could already feel the heat of the day.

There was a light rapping on the tinted window. "Five minutes, Senator."

Jane pressed a button, and the window rolled down. "Thank you, Sal."

She rolled the window back up and took out a mirror from her bag. Sapphire eyes stared back at her, and she wondered how she got here. How did she get from being an advocate for children's rights when she was fresh out of college to battling lobbyists in DC and now vying for the presidency? It wasn't something she ever wanted. She was perfectly happy with her old job working in a nonprofit agency years ago.

Then, she realized it had been Luke who encouraged her, gently pushing her down the path she was on.

She couldn't get Anita Duran's words out of her head. She glanced out the window at Luke. His handsome face drew in a small crowd of men and women around him, all wearing what was obviously custom business attire. He had always been charismatic.

*Angels and demons. I wonder if that's why he looks so young.*

She shook her head and laughed. She was letting her mind run away. It was nerves. That was all.

She powdered her nose and closed the compact with a click. *Okay, let's get this show on the road.*

Luke flashed a grin as she approached him.

"The stage is ready," Sal said from behind her.

"Wonderful." Luke offered her his arm. "Ready?"

"You bet." She placed her hand into the crook of his arm.

A wave of nausea hit her when she touched him.

"Are you sure? You look pale," he said.

Jane looked into his gray eyes. They looked back at her, cold. She blinked, and his eyes were back to their normal selves. "I...I think it's the heat."

"You there," Luke called to one of the stage crew.

The heavy-set man in the blue cap jogged to them. "Yes, Sir?" The man eyed Sal nervously, lowering his cap.

"Bring the senator some water, quickly."

"Yes, Sir."

"Mr. Prescott," Sal said. "I need a word with you."

"Not now," Luke said.

The young man returned and handed a bottle of water to Jane. "Thank you, uh, Mister..."

"Eduardo." He gave Sal a quick look and scurried off back to the stage.

Jane took a sip of the cold water. "That's better. I'm ready now...Luke?"

When she turned to Luke, he was whispering frantically with Sal. She looked around, panicked, wondering if there was a breach in security. She knew that her announcement wouldn't be popular with a lot of people, especially after the explosion incident. She feared someone would get hurt, trying to stop her.

A shadow passed over her, and she looked up. She felt a sickly chill as dark clouds gathered overhead. "Luke, maybe we should cancel or move this inside. It looks like a thunderstorm is coming."

"Nonsense. Nothing can stop your day of shining in the limelight. It's a new beginning for you, my dear."

Naomi let out a sigh of relief when Lalo joined Chuy and Megan on the opposite side of the stage from Sal and Lucifer. She wanted to get closer, but she kept her distance, hiding in a cluster of trees near an office building. Even though she was in her angel form and they weren't able to see her, she knew Lucifer and Sal could. She fought with every fiber in her being not to run over there and demand that they tell her where Lash was.

Thankful, for once, that angels had enhanced hearing abilities, she listened to them arguing about why Lalo was there. Lucifer looked nervously toward the group of reporters, who were starting to get curious. It was like they could pick up the scent of a scandal brewing.

She heard Lucifer order Sal to wait in the back of the crowd and to deal with Lalo later.

*Jeremy, where are you?* She couldn't let them get to Lalo. She knew she was there to watch over Megan, but if Sal touched a single hair on Lalo's head, she didn't care how powerful he was. He was going down.

"Ladies and Gentlemen." A Texas twang rang out through the audience when a middle-aged man wearing a tan Stetson spoke into the microphone. "As mayor of this fine town, I'd like to welcome you to Gardenville, Texas.

This is a historic moment in our country's history. It is the birth of a new party, the American Federation party. The AF will take this country by storm and forge for us a better and brighter future. It is my honor, my privilege, to introduce our fearless and dedicated leader, Texas' very own, Senator Jane Sutherland!"

There was polite applause as the senator approached the lectern. Naomi edged closer, her eyes darting between Megan and Chuy as the senator's voice boomed through the speakers.

"Thanks to all of you who braved the heat today. You are here because you believe that the American Federation can transform this nation, this country, into a better America."

As Jane spoke, Naomi watched Megan struggle to push her way past the security guards who blocked the entrance to the stage. The senator glanced in the direction of the disturbance but continued on with her speech. A few news reporters caught sight of what was happening and started making their way to the commotion.

A gust of wind rushed through the trees, sending a flock of birds screeching out into the darkening sky. Flashes of light lit the sky, and the audience grew nervous.

"Let go of me!" Megan tugged on a security officer who was dragging her away from the stage. "I have proof that Prescott Oil is illegally dumping the chemicals used in their drilling."

A small group of reporters swarmed to her, firing one question after another.

"What proof do you have?"

"Are you with Green Peace?"

"Are you with Texans Against Environmental Destruction?"

"Aren't you Megan Dalene, the niece of the woman who died in the gas leak accident?"

"It wasn't an accident. Prescott Oil is to blame for my aunt's death!" Megan cried over the thunder and wind. Her hair blew wildly, hitting against her face. "My little cousin was severely burned. She's only four years old."

"You're going to have to leave." A security guard grabbed her arm and hauled her away from the growing crowd of reporters.

"Leave her alone," Chuy growled, blocking the guard. "She has every right to be here."

"Step back," the security officer warned. He took out a walkie-talkie and called for police assistance.

"Take it, Chuy!"

He reached out to Megan's outstretched hand and took what looked like a USB flash drive. He then turned towards the stage.

The moment Chuy placed his foot on the step leading onto the stage, Naomi felt a surge of terror.

"Don't, Chuy!" Naomi ran to him, knowing he couldn't hear her but praying that maybe, just maybe he could sense her.

Then everything seemed to happen all at once.

From the corner of her eye, she saw Lucifer nod in her direction. She felt a jolt hit against her back, and she fell to the ground. Quickly, she flipped over, just as one of the evil twins was about to strike. She flicked out her wings and took off up into the sky, with the dark angel chasing after her.

There was another loud crack of thunder, and a stinging rain poured down. She was flying as fast as she could go, trying to out-maneuver the dark angel, when his twin appeared.

She stopped and hovered above the audience, who were scrambling to get out of the rain. With one dark angel on her right and the other to her left, she had no choice but to fight.

The dark angel to her left gave her a wicked smile. Just as he was about to attack, there was a loud crash, and he spiraled down to the ground with Jeremy on top of him.

Naomi quickly turned around, and the other dark angel slammed into her, placing an arm around her neck. She twisted and clawed his arm, trying to pull him off her.

She heard a scream in the crowd below. When she looked down, people were dropping to the ground. And that's when she saw Sal pull out a gun. He was aiming it at Chuy.

"No!" She wailed and bit into the dark angel's arm as hard as she could.

He screeched and released his hold, shouting a stream of obscenities.

Quickly, she flew down toward the stage. "Run, Chuy!"

Just as she was about to reach him, she felt a searing pain on her wing as the dark angel grabbed onto it. She watched helplessly as the dark angel jerked her back. She could see every single detail between Chuy and the senator as if it were all in slow motion.

The senator pushed her wet hair off her forehead and turned to Chuy, a look of recognition flashing across her face. She gazed down at his outstretched hand and was about to reach out to it when there was a loud crack.

She turned in the direction of the sound, her blue eyes widening at the sight of the gun. Her head turned, and her red lips formed a silent "No," as she looked to Chuy.

In one swoop, she pushed him away and fell back as the bullet lodged into her own chest.

"You fool!" Naomi heard Lucifer roar as he ran onto the stage.

"Chuy!" Naomi screamed, jerking herself forward.

A loud cackle of laughter from the dark angel was cut off by a loud bang, and she was suddenly free. She turned to face a grinning Uri.

"Go! I'll take care of Mr. Clean," he said.

Just then, Rachel emerged from the clouds with Raphael close behind her. His face was full of a rage she had never seen before and never thought possible from him.

He lifted his hand, and a fierce ray of light streaked down, striking Lucifer in the chest. His body flew back and landed on the edge of the stage. His suit was torn to shreds, exposing severe burns all over his body as he convulsed, rolling down the steps. When he landed on the bottom, his body fell limp, his eyes open and blank.

The dark twins and Sal stared down at the motionless body. Within seconds, they disappeared.

"Let's go," Jeremy said as he flew toward the stage.

Naomi and the others landed on the stage. "He's alright," she said with relief as she looked Chuy over. "He's not hurt."

She watched as Chuy rolled over and crawled to the senator. Blood blossomed on her suit.

"Senator. Hold on. I'll get you some help."

She grabbed his hand. "Tell...tell your grandmother..."

"Don't talk, Senator. Save your energy. Let's get an ambulance over here!" Chuy yelled.

"Tell your grandmother...she was right," she wheezed. She closed her eyes and winced. Rain slid down her pale face.

"Right about what? Senator? Senator?"

Slowly, she opened her eyes, and Naomi felt a pang in her chest as she watched the Senator's tears mix with the rain on her face. She didn't look like the powerful woman the world knew. She looked like a little girl, innocent, and pure. It was the Jane that Lash must've seen.

"How beautiful! He's so beautiful," Jane said.

Naomi turned, surprised that she was looking directly at Uri. "Rachel and I have this one, Jeremy. Go with Naomi and get Lash. Raphael will show you the way."

"Where are the others? Where are the rest of the angels?" Naomi cried to Raphael.

"There is no army for this." Raphael gazed sadly at her. "All who came here did so of their own will."

# 20

"This is it? Are you sure?" Naomi gazed at the familiar clear stream that ran through the lush landscape and the towering snow-capped mountains in the background. "This doesn't look like Hell. It looks like home."

"Lucifer purposely made it look like the home where the fallen came from," Raphael said as he stopped in front of a waterfall. "It makes it easier to sway those who are displeased with their work. It is not until after they join him that they realize the truth."

"Lash is in there?" She pointed to the cave hidden behind the rushing water.

"Yes."

"What are we waiting for?" Naomi rushed past Jeremy.

"Wait!" Raphael grabbed her arm. "This is no ordinary place."

"I know. Rachel told me about the Lake of Fire." She shivered at the image of Uri being held captive. Lash was there now. There was no time to waste. "Let's go."

Raphael tightened his hold on her. "This is not something to be taken lightly. Let me go first." He put his hand into the water. It splashed onto his hand, and he withdrew it, wincing.

"What is it?" Jeremy drew her behind him.

Raphael turned to them, a serious look in his eyes. "All that you see here—the water, the cave, even the air—is made to weaken you, body and soul. The closer you get to the lake, the more your powers will be stripped from you. Do not let the lava touch you. It *will* burn."

"I know that," she said. She didn't care what happened to her. She just wanted to get to Lash. "I'm ready."

"We must be careful, but we must also be swift. Lucifer can return at any time."

"What? But I saw you kill him," she said.

"You saw me destroy his human body, but his soul remains. We may have only moments before his soul is revived, and he'll head straight here to destroy us all."

With a deep breath, he turned and went through the water.

Naomi followed after him. When the water hit her back and wings, a searing pain hit the core of her being, and she threw a hand over her mouth, muffling her screams.

"Naomi!" Jeremy ran through the water, gritting his teeth as he went through.

Raphael drew her into his arms and gently glided his hand over her back. She immediately felt the pain turn into a dull ache.

Raphael leaned against the cave wall, gasping for air. "Jeremy, I am sorry. I won't be able to heal you right now. Give me a moment."

"Save your strength for Lash." Jeremy patted him on the shoulder. "I can take the pain."

Naomi ran down the tunnel as fast as she could, struggling to keep up with Raphael and Jeremy. The dull ache on her wings and back was nothing compared to the searing pain that swept through her lungs with each breath of the ice-cold air. Jeremy sprinted far ahead of them. She heard his groans echoing through the cave every couple of minutes. But he kept his pace, never slowing down.

Her feet were growing numb, and she barely felt the ground beneath her. She tripped, and Raphael caught her. "We are almost there, Naomi."

She nodded, gasping. She couldn't breathe. She needed air. But with each gasp, it was like she was swallowing a thousand knives, each one piercing her chest.

She expanded her wings and tried to take flight, hoping to get to Lash faster. Her wings felt like dead weights on her shoulders, and she could barely lift herself off the ground.

"Lash!" Jeremy's yell echoed down the corridor.

She felt her stomach drop at the despair in his voice, and with every ounce of strength she had, she propelled herself forward. Raphael followed close behind.

They entered into the vast chamber, and a wave of heat slammed into her, blurring her vision. She blinked until her eyes cleared. Across the lake of lava, tied against a cracking wall and charred almost beyond recognition was Lash.

"No!" She screamed hysterically and fell to the ground. Her hands clawed the cave floor as she wailed in agony. "No! No! No!"

*It's too late. We're too late.*

Her Lash, her beautiful Lash, hung limp and motionless against the stone wall. Chains around his wrists, waist, and feet were the only things that seemed to hold him up. Lava oozed from the cracks in the wall above him, dripping down onto his charred wings and body.

"Lash! Lash!" He can't be dead. He *can't* be dead. *I won't believe it!*

Her heart leapt into her throat as his head lifted slightly.

"Naomi," he croaked, his voice barely above a whisper.

"I'm coming!" she cried as she struggled to get to her feet. She'd gotten as far as the edge of the lake when lava shot through the air and splashed on her foot, making her stumble and fall to the ground, crying out in pain.

"Naomi," Lash's voice rasped. "Don't."

"Jeremy will get him." Raphael carried her away from the edge of the lake.

Naomi watched as Jeremy flew over the bubbling lava, his wings flapping heavily, his strained face growing red with the effort. She gasped as he dipped down, inches from the lava below. He grunted and pushed himself harder until finally he was at Lash's side.

"I have you, Brother." Taking hold of the chains, Jeremy winced in pain.

"Jeremy," Lash's voice whispered. "Forgive me."

"Don't talk like that. I'm getting you out of here so you can kick my ass again. You hear me? Hang on." Jeremy took a deep breath and let out a feral growl as he ripped the chains off the wall.

Naomi cried while she watched Jeremy's hands turn black as the chains burned into him.

"They will be fine," Raphael said, trying to comfort her. "I will see to their healing as soon as we are away from here. I promise."

She sighed with relief as the last chain was removed and Lash fell into Jeremy's arms. He grunted, and his wings flapped wildly as he tried to take flight.

"I can't fly with him!" Jeremy yelled to them from across the lake. "I'll have to walk the path."

She nervously eyed the narrow strip of rock. There was more lava than rock. It splashed against the path, washing over it.

Jeremy hitched Lash higher up into his arms and took a careful step onto the narrow sliver of stone. Molten liquid splashed onto his feet, and he gritted his teeth. Without a sound, he moved forward, one step at a time.

"Careful, my son." Raphael said.

Jeremy was half-way across when Naomi heard a sound coming from the tunnels behind them. Her heart dropped to the pit of her stomach. It was the fluttering of wings.

"Jeremy, they're coming! They're—" Iron hands gripped her by the throat and hurled her body into the air, slamming her against the wall of the cave.

Air rushed out of her, and she wheezed, trying to catch her breath. Her eyes widened as Sal approached her, his hulking body towering over hers, cold eyes ravishing her body.

"After I'm done with the others, we have some business to take care of." He smirked.

"Run, Naomi!" Raphael lunged at Sal.

She gasped as Sal punched Raphael, making him fall to the ground.

She scrambled to her feet, letting out her wings as far as they would go. She was chosen to be an archangel. She was trained to fight. Fight she would!

She screeched as she jumped on top of Sal's back. His wings flapped wildly as she dug her nails in, ripping into them.

With a roar, Sal reached out behind him and latched onto her hair. With a swift jerk, he threw her off him.

She panted on the rough ground of the cave and was about to attack again, when there was a loud clapping.

Lucifer stood at the chamber entrance, his eyes filled with amusement. "Impressive. I didn't know you had it in you, my dear Naomi. Pity that you and your *family*"—he sneered the word— "won't be around long enough to see what you would have become."

He held out his hand. The cave trembled, and the fiery liquid in the lake started to rise. She watched in horror as the lava drew closer to Jeremy and Lash.

She turned to Raphael, and their eyes locked in silent agreement. Then he let out a feral roar, and they both ran to attack Lucifer.

"Oh, no you don't." Sal growled as he tackled her, sending her body slamming against his chest. One of his hulking arms wrapped around her waist and the other around her throat. She clawed his arm as she felt herself being turned.

"You need to see this," he snarled. "Watch and learn the power of Lucifer, little girl."

With each blow, thunder reverberated through the chamber as Lucifer beat Raphael within an inch of his life. She shut her eyes in despair. She couldn't bear to watch him being savagely beaten.

Just when she thought she couldn't take any more, she heard Jeremy's sweet baritone voice, calm and soft. The words echoed in her ears, shattering her heart into a million pieces when she realized what the words meant.

"Yea, though I walk through the valley of the shadow of death, I will fear no evil, for You are with me."

Naomi's eyes flashed open, and she let out an agonizing cry. Jeremy's feet were slowly disappearing into the lava as he walked down the lava-covered path toward them. He held Lash tightly against his chest, protecting him from the splashes of the burning liquid.

He took another step, and his foot sank ankle deep into the lava. His beautiful face contorted. He paused, taking short and shallow breaths. Then he looked down at Lash, his face returning to a serene calm.

Tucking Lash closer to him, he kissed his charred forehead, and repeated the psalm under his breath as he moved onward.

When Jeremy's eyes found hers, she felt a surge of love from that simple look, his love for her, for Lash, for Raphael. He knew he was dying. He was doing it for his brother, and for her.

Sal's laughter echoed in the chamber, and hate boiled deep within her. A blinding rage filled her, and she clawed at Sal's arm. He growled in pain, throwing her down on the ground.

He lifted his foot and was about to kick her when a strong gust of wind followed by a blur of white rushed past her and knocked him down.

"Now, Rachel! Uri!" Gabrielle yelled, flying toward Jeremy and Lash.

In one swoop, Uri grabbed Sal, pummeling his fists into him. Each blow sounded with a thunderous roar.

Rachel helped Naomi up, and both ran to Raphael's aid. Lucifer shoved Raphael in their direction and sent him soaring in the air, striking them down.

Naomi jumped to her feet and was about to attack again when Lucifer held his hand up and a string of lava whipped out of the lake and singed her face, momentarily blinding her. She fell to the ground.

Everything seemed to slow down as her sight came back to her. She could see every feather of Gabrielle's snowy white wings as they flapped powerfully above Jeremy. He lifted Lash to her, and she took him gently into her arms. She gave a simple nod to Jeremy, and she went to Naomi.

The others held Lucifer and Sal off as Gabrielle laid Lash's charred body at her feet.

"Lash, my love." Naomi gently lifted him and cradled him in her arms, tears streaming down her face.

"Jeremy?" Lash's pained hazel eyes gazed back at her.

"Raphael will get him," she said.

Lash nodded and closed his eyes, passing out.

Naomi looked for Gabrielle and Raphael. They'd save Jeremy. Raphael could heal him. She knew he could.

Then her heart caught in her throat, horrified, when she looked to Jeremy. His body was slowly sinking into the lava.

She watched as Jeremy and Raphael locked eyes and silently communicated with each other. Jeremy's blue eyes glowed with resolve, and he gave Raphael a curt nod.

Grief swept over Raphael's face. He studied Jeremy, unable to tear his eyes away from him. Then finally, he returned the nod as if accepting his son's fate.

He turned to Gabrielle, his face a mask of determination. "Now!"

Together, they charged at Lucifer, their feet slamming against his chest and sending him toward Jeremy. Jeremy reached and grabbed hold of his ankle before Lucifer could regain control.

With a savage roar, he plunged them both into the fiery lake.

# 21

Screams echoed in Lash's ears. *Jeremy! Jeremy!*

His heart pounded frantically against his chest as he searched for his brother in the darkness.

*Where are you?* He had to find him—to tell him that he was wrong. To tell him that he understood.

He moved faster and faster, getting nowhere. His legs felt like they were moving through an ocean of wet sand as he struggled forward.

*I need to tell him. I need to...before it's too late.*

Searing heat slammed against his chest, and he felt himself falling.

Falling.

Falling.

"Jeremy!" He shouted as he jerked up.

"Lash, it's okay." Soft hands touched his arm. "You're home."

He looked into Naomi's pale blue eyes and then gathered her against his chest. "Naomi. You're safe."

He kissed her forehead, her cheeks, and the salty tears that streamed down her face. "You shouldn't have gone after me. You could have...could have..." He couldn't even say the words.

She drew back and cupped his face tenderly. "There is nothing, I mean, nothing, that will ever keep me away from you again. I love you. Always."

He kissed her deeply, his tears blending with hers. Fingers weaved into her hair, relishing the soft waves. He was never going to let her go again. Never.

Her soft hands delicately brushed his back, and he winced.

"Does it hurt? Raphael, come quick."

Raphael hurried into the room and sighed as he inspected Lash. "You're recovering nicely."

"His back hurts," Naomi said.

"Just a little, my love." He squeezed her shoulder.

Raphael sat on the chair next to the bed. "That's to be expected. I was able to heal everything, including your wings. There will be some minor discomfort for a while." His face turned solemn. "Lash, about Jeremiel..."

Lash's throat grew thick. "Did you heal him, too?"

He felt his soul grow numb as he heard Naomi's heart-wrenching sob. She buried her head in his chest.

He swallowed. "Raphael?"

Raphael's blue eyes, so much like Jeremy's, looked up at him filled with torment. "Jeremiel...Jeremiel is...dead."

He moaned, dropping his head onto Naomi's shoulder. "Not Jeremy. Please not Jeremy. Why? Why?"

He rocked with Naomi as they clung to each other, crying an endless river of tears.

"It should have been me," he sobbed. "It should have been me! He's the good one."

"No, Lahash." He felt Raphael place a firm hand on his shoulder. "Both of you are good. It was my fault that you grew up believing otherwise. Jeremiel loved you deeply as a friend and a brother. He didn't think twice about going after you, and neither did I. My son, can you forgive me for all my wrongdoing?"

Lash placed a hand over Raphael's. He remembered Lucifer's words. Raphael wasn't his father. He didn't care. Raphael was always there for him, just as Jeremy was. Raphael was his true father.

"I forgive you, Raphael. I forgive Jeremy. You are my family."

It was at that moment when a surge of images flashed through his mind, memories of him and Jeremy as small boys, running up a grassy hill together, playing; memories of sitting on Rebecca's lap in front of a stone fire place, singing to him; memories of meeting Naomi by a stream, of them falling in love.

Naomi gasped, and she looked up at him, her eyes shining. "I remember. I remember you and Jeremy. You were different but the same. How is that possible? What happened?"

"What do you remember?" Raphael asked.

"I remember I had another family." She gazed off in the distance, her eyes shifting back and forth as if watching a movie in her mind. "My father owned an inn in the City of Ai. And there were little girls...I had sisters!"

"I remember, too," Lash said. "Your sisters would follow us when we snuck off into the hills. I remember my life. I remember my mother and you...Father." He smiled at Raphael.

"Why?" Naomi asked. "Why now? What happened?"

Tears welled in Raphael's eyes. "I believe it is because Lahash has truly forgiven me and accepted me for who I am." He wrapped his arms around both of them. "He has brought you back to me."

Lash felt a peace within him grow under Raphael's fatherly love, but there was an empty place in his heart. His brother was gone.

Time passed. Lash drifted in and out of sleep with Naomi lying next to him and Raphael sitting by his bedside watching over him. He couldn't get himself out of bed, and he didn't want to.

It was all one big blur for him as he held onto Naomi. At one point, he heard Raphael whisper in hushed tones that he was leaving to visit a little redheaded girl in the hospital and that Jeremy would have wanted him to do so.

Grief washed over him in dark waves, and he could feel Naomi's sorrow, too. Sometimes it was small and lulling, almost bearable. At other times it was large and overwhelming, and the only thing that kept him from drowning in it was Naomi's soft crooning that she loved him. All he could do was hold on tight to her until the tide of grief pulled back, making his waking hours just a little bit bearable again.

He had no idea how long they stayed hidden in the refuge of their bedroom, holding each other. Daylight shone through the open windows, and in the blink of an eye darkness fell. Day turned to night and night into day. He lost count of how many, and he didn't care. As long as Naomi was by his side, he didn't care if the entire world came to an end, because his already had.

Slowly over time, he didn't know how long, they started to share their newfound memories of each other and of Jeremy. They laughed. They cried, and gradually the ache, the absence of him, wasn't as painful.

There was a knock at the door, and Lash groaned. "Tell them to go away."

Rachel's voice came from the other side of the door. "I hear you, Lash, and I'm not going away. Don't make me break the door down."

"I think she means it, Lash." Naomi hopped out of the bed.

"Alright." He huffed, walking to the door. When he reached it, he swung it open. "Rachel, I'm not ready for poker with Uri right—"

He froze, surprised to find Gabrielle standing beside Rachel.

"I was afraid you wouldn't open the door if you knew it was just me," she said.

"Gabrielle. Rachel." Naomi ran to his side. "Please come in. Have a seat."

They sat in the living room in awkward silence. He knew he should say something to Gabrielle. It was just so hard to believe that she'd gone after him and risked her own life to save him.

"Uh, Gabrielle, I...uh, I need to... thank..."

She held up a hand. "No, Lash. I know what you want to say, and it's not necessary. Actually, I'm here on other business."

"I'm here on official business, too." Rachel chimed in. "I don't know if you realized this, but you two have been in here for weeks. We've all been mourning Jeremy. Believe me, I know what it feels like. But Jeremy wouldn't want you to be like this. He gave his life for you," She looked at Lash. "And he wanted you to be together," she said to Naomi.

"I know that," he said softly.

Naomi placed her hand in his. "We both know that, and we love him even more for it."

"I spoke with Michael, and he's agreed to do the binding ceremony. I think we should do that. And you know Jeremy would have wanted you to do it."

Lash looked at Naomi. Her face beamed with happiness for the first time since they lost Jeremy. "You're right. We should have the binding ceremony."

"Good. See, that wasn't so hard." Rachel got up from the sofa and skipped to the door.

"The ceremony's next week," she sang.

He balked. "Next week?"

Rachel turned. "Too soon?"

"I don't think it's too soon," Naomi said.

He looked into her eyes and brushed a hand over her cheek. She'd been through so much. She deserved happiness right now. They both did.

"No, it's not."

Rachel squealed. "I can't wait to tell Uri. He thought Lash was going to freak. He was so wrong. See you in the morning. Oh, I have so much to prepare," she said as the door closed behind her.

"As I was saying." Gabrielle continued as if she hadn't been interrupted. "I'm here on business. After discussing it with Michael, we felt that you both deserved to know what has transpired since you've been…on leave."

Naomi raised an eyebrow. It was obvious to Lash what she was thinking. She probably thought Gabrielle was avoiding the subject of Jeremy's death. She wasn't used to Gabrielle's word choice, especially when it came to touching on something so personal like grief. As always, Gabrielle was all business.

Lash thought they would have bonded over the experience of her saving his life, that perhaps she would be more personable with them. He sighed, apparently not.

"Chuy and Welita, are they okay?"

Gabrielle turned to Naomi. "Yes. I've taken the liberty of checking in on them for you. You can look in on them from the bridge any time you wish."

He did a double take. Gabrielle was just full of surprises.

"Thank you," Naomi sighed with relief. "I was worried that Sal would go after Chuy, especially since...Jeremy...was assigned to him." The name caught in her throat.

"You're correct in your assumption, Naomi. Jeremy was there to escort your cousin after his death."

Naomi gasped and squeezed Lash's hand. "Chuy's not still... he's not going to..."

"He's not in danger of dying anytime soon. That all changed with Jane Sutherland."

"Jane? What happened to her?" Lash asked.

"Saleos was about to kill Naomi's cousin, and Jane pushed him out of the way. She sacrificed her own life for his. It was her selfless act that changed everything that followed after," she explained.

He couldn't believe it. He was so sure Jane Sutherland was on Lucifer's side.

"She believed Welita. I know she did. And you were right, Lash. There was good in her," Naomi choked. "You saw it when no one else did."

"There is good in all, Naomi," Gabrielle said softly. "Everyone is given free will to choose which path they'll follow. She chose with her heart and was willing to give up all the worldly power that Lucifer bestowed on her."

"What about the man people know as Luke Prescott?" Lash wondered how they would handle it now that Lucifer was gone.

"Luke Prescott died by being struck by lightning. It's not common, but it's been known to happen." She turned to Naomi. "It may be of interest to you to know that the news media did get a hold of the evidence that Eduardo managed to steal."

"Eduardo?" he asked.

"She means Lalo," Naomi said.

"Yes, him. The girl, Ms. Dalene, was given some type of settlement for the death of her aunt. And as for the shooter, law enforcement is still looking for him. Saleos is gone for now, but Michael will keep a look-out for him."

Gabrielle stood. "Well, that's all the information I have to share with you. And Naomi, we can resume your training as soon as you're ready."

"Uh, I wanted to talk to you about that. I was wondering if..." Naomi bit on her lip. "Uh, I don't know how to say this."

Gabrielle arched an eyebrow. "I think I know what you're going to say."

"You do?"

Lash looked at Naomi, puzzled. "What's going on?"

"She doesn't want to be an archangel."

Naomi let out a breath. "Yes. I mean, it's just not for me. I'd rather be a seraph like Lash. I don't know if that's possible. Is it?"

Lash watched Gabrielle's lips curl into a smile, and his jaw dropped at the sight of it.

"Being an archangel is not for everyone." She threw him a glance. "And I believe you are more suited to work as a seraph. I'll talk to Michael. I'm sure he'll agree."

Naomi stood and escorted Gabrielle to the door. "I'm so relieved. I thought I'd have to be an archangel forever."

"We all have a choice, Naomi. That doesn't change when you become an angel." And with that, she walked out the door.

# 22

"Lash is doing better, Welita. I know he's just as excited as I am about the binding ceremony this afternoon. And I can't believe I'm finally going to meet Michael. I've been hearing about him all this time, and I still haven't met him. He's going to conduct the ceremony. Oh, and Gabrielle came by early this morning and told me that Michael agreed that I can be a seraph and work with Lash."

Looking over the bridge and watching Welita rocking in a chair on the porch of her new home, Naomi sighed. She'd been to the bridge every day since Gabrielle's visit. "Everything is finally coming together, and I'm so happy. I just wish I could help Lash let go of some of his guilt about what happened with Jeremy. I don't think anyone could except for Jeremy, himself. Oh Welita, I miss him so much. We all do."

She watched Welita look up into the sky and smile. She knew Welita could feel her presence. It was a happy day for Naomi, the first since losing Jeremy. Part of her wondered if the ache in her would ever go away. As Rachel said, Jeremy would've wanted them to be happy. She was right. The world moves on, even when all you want to do is crawl into bed and stay in there forever.

Bear padded slowly to Welita, which made Naomi frown. The poor girl was getting old. She wondered what happened to animals when they died. She ached with the thought that Welita might be losing Bear soon, knowing how much she loved that dog.

She smiled as Chuy jogged up the porch steps and scooped Bear up with one hand. Turning, he handed her to a little girl with strawberry curls and a splattering of freckles on her nose. "Here you go, Little Orphan Annie. Take Bear inside with you."

"My name's not Annie; it's Emma. Megan," she whined. "Chuy's calling me Annie again."

Naomi chuckled and shook her head. She didn't think she'd ever get used to the fact that Chuy married Megan. After the shooting, Chuy and Megan became inseparable. She didn't know what to think about that. She'd never seen him so taken by a girl before. It wasn't until he took Megan to meet Welita that Naomi saw that he had fallen head over heels in love with her. He'd never taken anyone to meet their grandmother.

In broken Spanish, Megan spoke to Welita. Naomi was impressed and touched that Megan would learn another language just for her grandmother. She could tell that Welita loved it.

It was when Megan was shown a photo of Naomi and Chuy that Naomi really started to like her. How could she not like someone who called her the most beautiful girl she'd ever seen? Megan even blushed with embarrassment when she was told that Naomi and Lash were an item.

That made Naomi smile.

When Naomi first saw that Chuy and Megan were about to marry, she thought it was too quick. They hardly knew each other. Then she remembered the time difference between Earth and Heaven and had a change of heart, especially now that Megan was eight months pregnant.

"Chuy, stop teasing her." Megan slapped his arm playfully. "Welita, come inside. It's too hot to be out."

Welita looked into the sky and waved. Naomi waved back. Thanks to Megan and Emma, she felt a sense of peace, knowing that Welita would be spending her last days surrounded by those who loved her.

"I'm just having a little chat with my Naomi. She's happy today," Welita said as Chuy helped her out of her chair.

"Blow her a big kiss for me, Welita," Megan said as she ushered Emma into the house.

Naomi laughed. "Back at you, Megan."

She felt a pair of strong arms wrap around her waist, and she sighed.

"Having a good visit?" Lash's warm breath caressed her ear.

"Mmm, hmm." She leaned back into his chest.

"Did you tell her?" His nose glided down her neck, creating a ripple of goose bumps at his touch.

"Yes," she said breathlessly. She loved it when he did that to her. It was a feeling she would never get tired of.

He turned her around and with a finger under her chin, lifted her face to look up at him. "Any reservations?"

Light hazel eyes searched her face, and she knew that he meant more than the binding ceremony.

She took his hand into hers. "It took me a while to adjust to being here. It wasn't easy."

"And now?"

"I'm not saying it's easier. I don't think it ever will be. But one thing I know for sure. Whatever challenge I face in serving my role as a seraph, I know that with you by my side, we can accomplish anything."

"Even with Gabrielle as your supervisor?" He smirked. "You could be your own boss if you were an archangel. It's not too late to change your mind."

"Yes, even with her. And I'm not changing my mind. And you"—she poked his chest— "need help in your work relationship with Gabrielle. Is there some kind of angel employee assistance program here? You could use some counseling."

He chuckled. "Okay, okay. She's not that bad."

"Not 'that bad'? She saved your life."

He let out a playful grumble. "Hey, I did invite her to the binding ceremony."

"Yes, you did. And I'm so proud of you for that." She got on her tiptoes and pecked his nose. "What about you? Getting cold feet?"

His beautiful face grew serious, and his eyes looked deeply into hers. "Naomi, I've waited for you for centuries. Nothing is going to stop me from making you mine."

## 23

Rays of light filtered into the Room of Offerings, dancing on the statuettes that lined the shelves. Lash picked one up. It was shaped in Jeremy's likeness. He was thankful that it had survived his previous bout of destruction because it was the only reminder of Jeremy he had left.

At the time, when he thought he'd never see Naomi again, he had wanted to break everything in sight. He'd been so angry at all of them—Jeremy, Raphael, and Gabrielle—for keeping secrets and taking Naomi away from him. He had blamed them all. He hadn't known they were actually bringing Naomi back to him.

"I miss you, my friend. I can't get out of my head the horrible things I said to you. I wish I could take them back." He fingered Jeremy's likeness. It was perfection in his hands: perfect face, perfect smile, perfect body. He was like others had claimed him to be—a god among men. And Lash didn't care, not anymore.

"I understand the love you have for Naomi. I didn't at first." He shook his head. "I was so jealous and...afraid."

His voice dropped to a whisper. "Everyone loved you, worshipped you. In their eyes, you could do no wrong. And me?"

He let out a sigh. "I was the exact opposite. It didn't bother me before. It wasn't until I had something, someone I wanted, that I even noticed. When I saw that you loved her, I thought that you wanted her, that you wanted to take her away from me. I was wrong."

He placed the statuette back onto the shelf and closed the glass door. He pressed a hand and forehead against the cool glass, not wanting to leave the only thing that was a part of Jeremy.

"Why did it take losing you to know that you're one of the best things to happen in my life? I had you and Raphael with me all those years, and I took you for granted. And now, on the day I'm to be bound with Naomi"—his voice croaked, and he swallowed thickly—"you won't be by my side, and I want you there. I *need* you there with me...by my side...One. More. Time."

Lash paced beneath a large white cherry tree in the garden, brushing a hand through his thick locks. Uri, who was to stand by his side during the ceremony, snickered each time he passed him.

Lash threw him a glare. He was not helping the situation. Was this what people meant by cold feet? He hadn't thought he was going to be nervous. Where was she? She'd probably come to her senses and was hiding out somewhere.

He heard approaching footsteps, and he whirled around. "Oh," he said, looking disappointed when Raphael and Gabrielle came into view.

Gabrielle frowned. "Why does that not surprise me?"

"I didn't mean it like that. It's just...I...oh, never mind." He threw up his hands and continued to pace.

Raphael chuckled. "He's a bit nervous, Gabrielle. I'm sure he means nothing by it. Lash, Michael will be here shortly."

Lash nodded as he continued to pace, wringing his hands.

"Lash," Uri said under his breath as he walked with him. "If you want to make a fast getaway, I can tell Gabrielle about the secret stash of Cuban cigars, and we can get you booted out again." He grinned, waggling his eyebrows.

He stopped and glared at Uri. "Not helping, man."

"Uri, stop teasing him." Rachel's soprano voice echoed from a distance.

Lash turned around and gasped. Naomi was a vision to behold. White fluttered around her as she walked to him wearing a delicate white dress that fell to her ankles. It was a simple dress with pink roses that lined the collar and around her waist. Dark hair fell down in soft waves onto her shoulders. Her cheeks were tinted pink, and pale blue eyes danced with excitement. She was dazzling. His heart ached at the sight of her.

"You came," he breathed when she took her place at his side.

She looked at him, surprised. "Of course I did."

Lash leaned over to kiss her, but instead, his lips pressed up against a large palm.

"Uh-uh, my friend," Uri said, his hand acting as a barrier between his and Naomi's lips. "After the binding ceremony."

He growled and wiped his mouth. "Do you mind with the hand, Uri?"

"I see Uriel is still up to his old tricks."

There was no mistaking Archangel Michael's deep, majestic voice. The last time Lash had seen him was in the dimness of the Hall of Judgment thirty-five years ago.

He watched Michael's smiling face greet Raphael. Michael looked exactly the same as when he last saw him. Same dark curly hair and serious brown eyes. Except today those eyes turned to him with pride.

"Michael, this is my Naomi," he said, puffing out his chest.

"Naomi. It is an honor for me to be performing the binding ceremony." Michael took her hand and kissed it.

"Oh, no, Michael...er, Archangel...Sir," she stammered, looking at him in awe. "It is our honor to have you with us."

"You can call me Michael. And believe me, it is always a joyous occasion for me when there is a binding ceremony, and especially so for Lahash and Raphael. Much has happened to their family over the centuries. Much, much heartbreak that for many would have been unbearable. But there was good in their hearts, so they persevered, even after the losses."

Lash swallowed thickly as he glanced over at Raphael. He knew he was thinking about Jeremy, too and maybe even Rebecca. If anyone deserved Michael's praise, it was Raphael. Not only had he lost his son, he'd been without the love his life by his side for centuries.

It was hard to believe that Lash would ever think that having his memories suppressed was a good thing. He'd only met Rebecca once, but in that brief time he could understand how difficult it must've been for Raphael to be away from her.

"Raphael, you have been a true and faithful servant," Michael said. "Your loyalty has not gone unnoticed. And Lahash"—he turned his attention to him—"your ability to love deeply, to forgive, is what makes you special and loved by all. Both of you have earned the gift I bring to you today."

He gestured behind them, and Lash turned in the direction he was pointing.

A light breeze went through the trees, sending a flurry of white blossoms into the air. Then there was a shimmering blur in the middle of the garden as if the air was beginning to solidify. White petals whirled around the shimmer like a spiral, spinning faster and faster, until the blur divided in two.

"Lash, what is *that?*" Naomi whispered.

"I don't know."

He blinked, and one of the blurs started to take shape. Feet, legs, torso, all began to appear. Then slowly, the image became clearer—small, slender, curves, long dark hair, hazel eyes.

Raphael gasped. "Rebecca!"

Rebecca blinked, her eyes filling with tears as she looked at Raphael. She ran to him and threw herself into his arms. "Raphael, my husband, my love."

Raphael kissed every inch of her face. "Rebecca, my Rebecca. They have brought you back to me. At long last, you are here with me."

Lash's heart ached as he watched his father reunite with his mother. Naomi took his hand and squeezed it. Looking down at her, he saw that her eyes glistened and her pink lips curled into a smile. "They're beautiful together."

"Yes, they are," he said.

"You are the image of your mother," she whispered. "I can't get over how much alike you two look."

A movement from the corner of his eye caught his attention. It was Gabrielle, and the look on her face shocked him. It was a mixture of happiness, acceptance, and...longing. And that's when he finally realized that she was in love with Raphael. Maybe, somewhere deep inside, he'd always known that. Now it was clear on her face for everyone to see.

*You are the image of your mother.* Naomi's voice echoed in his mind.

That was it! That was why Gabrielle could barely stand to look at him. He reminded her of Rebecca, the woman Raphael loved.

He looked to Gabrielle, and for the first time, he felt like he could understand her. If it had been Naomi and Jeremy, he didn't know how he would've been able to handle their children. It also explained why she preferred Jeremy. He was exactly like Raphael.

"Lash! Look!" Naomi tugged his sleeve.

He turned to look at the remaining shimmering blur as it twisted and formed into shape: tall, broad shoulders, muscular arms.

His heart slammed into his chest, hoping against all hope as he stared at the shimmering blur. *Please, please, let it be him.*

Golden hair, sapphire eyes, Raphael's eyes...Jeremy's eyes gazed back at him.

Naomi gasped and covered a hand over her mouth. Wet eyes glanced between Lash and Jeremy.

His face was blank as he leaned down and kissed her. "I love you."

Turning, he marched up to Jeremy and stopped a foot away from him.

The garden was silent as Jeremy stood looking intently at Lash, his face stoic.

"Brother," Lash croaked, throwing his arms around him.

Tears streamed down his face as Jeremy embraced him. "I'll never forsake you again."

"Nor I you, my brother," Jeremy whispered into his ear.

"Jeremy!" Naomi squealed as she threw herself at the both of them.

In that brief moment, embraced by both Naomi's and Jeremy's arms, he could feel the love they had for him. It was a moment he'd always cherish and never forget. This was life's purpose, the secret to happiness: love and family. He'd never been happier in his entire life.

Jeremy snickered as he pulled back. Placing one arm around Naomi and the other around Lash, he said, "What's with the tear fest? A binding ceremony is supposed to be a joyous occasion. Now, when *yours truly* has a ceremony, that's when the water works will really be going full blast—for losing a stud like me."

He winked at Naomi and ruffled Lash's hair. "Let's get this party started."

# 24

This moment—standing in front of Archangel Michael with Lash by her side and family and friends watching—was more than Naomi had ever hoped for. In the back of her mind, she knew that somehow Welita, Chuy, and her parents were there with her. As long as she carried them in her heart, in her memories, they were never far away.

Every time she looked at Lash, her heart caught in her throat, leaving her breathless. He was heart-wrenchingly handsome. For the first time since she met him, he'd dressed up different from the usual T-shirt and jeans. His face glistened against the black of the tux, and his cheeks flushed a delicate pink with excitement. She fought the urge to weave her fingers into his silky dark hair and brush her cheek against his clean-shaven jaw.

"Naomi, place your hand into Lahash's. Raphael will bind you together as I perform the ceremony." Michael handed Raphael a thickly braided gold cord.

Raphael's face was a sea of emotion as he slowly wrapped the cord around Naomi's arm and then onto Lash's.

Michael's voice was deep and melodic as he repeated the words of the ceremony. Words that were centuries old. So beautiful, she would remember them always. "Naomi. Lahash. As Raphael binds you together, remember the hands that you are holding are those of your best friend."

He paused and gazed at her. "They are the hands of your husband."

Then turning to Lash he said, "And of your wife."

Lash gently squeezed her hand, smiling as Michael continued. "They are hands that will cherish you even when you are at your lowest. They will hold you as you cry and laugh together in your triumphs and failures. They are the hands of the one you will share your innermost secrets with, and who will always be there for you, even when all others have left."

A lump caught in her throat as Lash gazed deeply into her eyes. He had already done all that Michael had mentioned. Memories fluttered through her mind: Lash laughing with her around Welita's table; embracing her in the New Mexico hotel room while she cried; holding back her hair when she was sick, even when she tried to push him away. He'd always been there by her side.

"The binding cord represents the love that binds you together," Michael continued. "A love that began centuries ago, that not even Time itself could sever from your hearts."

Naomi heard someone blowing his nose loudly, followed by a "that's so beautiful" in a thick Russian accent.

"Naomi and Lahash have their own vows that they would like to say to each other. Naomi?"

She nodded at Michael and then took a nervous breath as she gazed deeply into Lash's hazel eyes. Warmth filled her heart, feeling the love coming from him and all around her. This was the Heaven she had wanted. She had a family who she loved on Earth, and now she had a second family here. She could see herself living here for all eternity with them, and that's why she said her vows not only to Lash but also to his family.

"Lash, I love you. I'll tell you 'I love you' every single day and never get tired of saying it. Without you, my heart would go on beating, but my soul would stop living. I give you my heart freely and make you my heart's protector. And I promise to hold and cherish your heart, too. I know I'm a little stubborn..."

He raised an eyebrow.

"Okay, I'm hard-headed. We'll more than likely disagree about things and argue, but always remember..." She cupped his face with her free hand. "I'll always be by your side loving you, even when I'm angry. I promise to listen to not only to your words, but to your heart. I promise I won't run away."

Tears wet his dark lashes, and his Adam's apple bobbed as he swallowed.

"We'll battle the good times and the bad, together." She paused, taking a deep breath before she continued, her voice quivering. "Lash, I've never felt closer to God than I do when I'm with you. With you, I've learned about faith and forgiveness. I once thought angels were perfect. We're not. But you and I, we are perfect together."

She gazed deeply into his eyes, eyes she could drown in forever, and whispered, "I love you."

"I love you." His voice was raw with emotion.

Michael cleared his throat and turned his red-rimmed eyes to Lash. "Lahash?"

Lash nodded and took a folded piece of paper out of his pocket. "I wrote something down." His hand shook as he tried to open it with his free hand. "I wanted to make sure I did this right. You deserve the best."

He dropped the paper, and his eyes widened. "I'm sorry."

He bent down to pick it up, and she stopped him. "You don't need that. Just say what's in your heart."

"I want you to have the best."

"I already do."

He bit down on his lip as tears lined his eyes. "Naomi," his voice shook. "I lived most of my life with a closed heart, never letting anyone in. And then you came into my life. Because of you, I've opened my heart, not only to you, but to family and friends. I thank the Heavens that you were brought back to me because..." He swallowed thickly.

"Because with you, I not only have the love of my life, but I have my family back, too. It's because of you that I've found the strength, the courage to love again. You...you set me free, and I'm... I'm no longer afraid."

Hot tears slid down her cheeks as Lash's voice sailed into her heart.

"Naomi, your love makes me have courage. It makes me want to be a better man because...because..." Tears flowed down his sweet face, and his voice squeaked with intense emotion. "Because even when I make mistakes, you still love me. Even when I sound like I just inhaled helium and am talking like Alvin the chipmunk, you still love me."

Naomi giggled, and laughter filled the garden. He was so funny. God, she loved him.

He brushed the tears from his eyes with the back of his sleeve and took a deep breath. His face turned serious, and he gazed into her eyes again. "No matter how much I stumble, I know you'll always be there for me, to pick me up. Naomi, you are the woman of my dreams, my memories, memories that I carried in my heart, my soul. Even when my memories were hidden from me, you were always there on the edges of my mind, never forgotten.

"I can't promise I won't screw up again or that I won't make you mad. But I can promise to love you with every fiber of my being. And I promise to always stand by your side, holding your hand as we take on whatever the future gives us."

He reached to her, and his thumb gently brushed the tears from her cheeks. Leaning in closer, his breath caressed her lips as he whispered, "I'm forever bound to you, my love. My Naomi. My angel."

She closed her eyes as he pressed his lips against hers, kissing them tenderly. And when she opened them, she saw Heaven in his eyes.

# EPILOGUE

"Lash, will you hand me the pot holders?" Naomi bent down and looked at the enchiladas. They looked about right. She was trying Welita's recipe tonight. She was not the best cook and had no idea how they would turn out. Luckily, the only one who had tasted Welita's awesome cooking was Lash. So she didn't have to worry about comparisons.

A hand slapped her behind, and she yelped. "Lash! What are you doing?"

He pressed himself against her. "What do you think?"

His hands stroked her bottom and then worked their way to the front. She quickly turned around. "Everyone will be here in a few minutes."

Feverish lips pressed down on hers, his tongue caressing the inside of her mouth. He nipped and sucked on her bottom lip as his hand stroked the back of her neck.

She melted.

When he pulled back, his eyes sparkled with mischief. "You were saying?"

"Family...potholders...dinner. What?"

He chuckled and waved the potholders. "Allow me."

"Lash, really. You have to stop doing that."

He took out the pan of enchiladas and placed it on the counter. "Oh, you want me to stop?"

"Well, not stop. Just not right before company's coming over. Wait until after they're gone."

He drew her against his chest, and she moaned as she felt him—hard, strong—and she thought of all the naughty things they could be doing at that moment. Maybe she could call the dinner off. Maybe tell them she was sick.

Damn! She couldn't do that. Angels don't get sick.

"What about during? I can think of some interesting ways to entertain ourselves. Where's the tablecloth? We'll need some coverage."

"Lash! Your parents will be at the table!"

"That just means we'll have to be extra sneaky, and you'll need to control yourself." He waggled his eyebrows. "Besides, we're newlyweds. They expect us to do things like this."

Her jaw dropped, and he gave her a wink.

"Ha, ha. Very funny," she said, shaking her head.

There was a knock at the door.

"Set the table. I'll get it," he said.

Rachel, Uri, and Jeremy stepped into the house, followed by Raphael and Rebecca.

"So, what's for dinner tonight?" Uri asked as everyone took a seat around the table.

"My grandmother's enchiladas," Naomi said.

"She makes the best enchiladas," Rebecca said as Raphael held out a chair out for her.

"You had some? I thought you were watching over her in your angel form," Raphael looked at her, surprised.

Rebecca's face turned pink. "I may have cheated a little. Do you blame me? It smells delicious."

There was another knock at the door, and Lash turned to Naomi. "You invited someone else?"

"Gabrielle. I hope you don't mind."

He leaned over and pecked her on the cheek. "Of course not."

She went to the door while Lash entertained their guests. As soon as Gabrielle stepped in, there was a loud yapping from the back of the house that headed in their direction.

"Bear, knock it off," Naomi said as Bear circled Gabrielle, barking.

Bear crouched in front of Gabrielle and growled.

Gabrielle threw her a glare, and Bear scuttled out of the room.

"Sorry about that," Naomi said.

*What in the world has gotten into that crazy dog?* Naomi shook her head.

When she heard Lash in the background saying "good dog," she rolled her eyes. Some things just never changed.

When Bear died, Naomi was distraught that she'd never see her again. Even though she was Welita's dog, Naomi and Lash had grown to love the little mutt. Then one day when she was standing on the bridge checking in on Welita, Jeremy came with Bear in his arms. He had asked special permission to bring her as a belated gift for them.

After dinner, everyone sat around listening to Uri telling stories about his human life in Chernobyl. Lash was unusually quiet as the animated Uri talked about his obsession with the new wave band, A Flock of Seagulls. He didn't even a say a word when Uri and Jeremy got into an argument about *I, Ran* being the best song of the decade.

She could feel that something was up when all Lash did was look over at Rebecca and Raphael. She wondered if he was thinking what she was.

After the binding ceremony, most of their time was spent lying in each other's arms, taking strolls in the gardens, and playing with Bear. They rarely talked about their experience in the Lake of Fire. Although, she was curious about whether or not Lucifer would ever return. She figured if Jeremy was able to, then why not Lucifer.

"Um, Raphael. I was wondering something."

"Oh, wait, Naomi," Uri said. "I haven't gotten to the good part yet, about Rachel getting a tattoo in 1986."

Rachel spit out the coffee she was sipping. "They don't want to hear about that."

"I do!" Jeremy leaned forward. "Where is it?"

Gabrielle rolled her eyes and muttered under her breath. "Jeremy."

"Not there!" Rachel slapped his hands away when he tried to lift her shirt. "Uri, we've monopolized the conversation enough already. Go ahead, Naomi."

"I was just wondering. Is it possible for Lucifer to return? Not that I want him to or anything. It's just that if Jeremy and Uri were able to return, then what about Lucifer?"

The room grew still as all eyes turned to Raphael.

"It is not up to us to decide if Lucifer does or does not return. Do not forget, the fallen still walk the Earth, and so does Saleos."

Uri snorted. "That coward? He flew like a bat out of Hell as soon as Jeremy took Lucifer out. See what I did there?" He directed to Rachel. "Bat out of Hell? I did a funny, no?"

"Yes, yes. Very funny." Rachel patted his knee.

"What if he does come back? You're short by one archangel." Naomi started to feel a little guilty about turning down the job.

Raphael smiled. "It's true you were the seventh archangel. But there are others who can fill the role." He threw a glance at Rebecca. "Just as Jeremiel started as a seraph and moved up in rank, so can others, if they wish."

He looked at Naomi again. "Lucifer was after you not only because of your potential as an archangel but because of Lash's love for you."

Naomi nodded. She shuddered as she remembered Sal's words. Lucifer basically used her as bait to get Lash to join him.

"I have a question about Lucifer," Lash said in a soft voice. "And about...Mom."

"Uh, Uri, Gabrielle, I think it's time for us to leave now. Don't you?" Rachel stood. "Thank you for having us, Naomi. Lash. Come on, Uri." She tugged his arm.

"But I want to hear the question," Uri whined.

"No, don't leave. Please stay," Rebecca said.

"Are you sure, Rebecca?"

Naomi looked at Gabrielle, shocked. This was the first time she'd heard Gabrielle address Rebecca. She knew Gabrielle was uncomfortable around her and that it was a small miracle she agreed to come to the dinner knowing Rebecca was going to be there. Naomi knew part of it was because Gabrielle had feelings for Raphael. Lash had told her he thought Gabrielle was in love with Raphael.

She looked around the room, and except for Jeremy, Lash, and herself, it seemed like everyone knew where the conversation was going.

"Yes, I'm sure." Rebecca placed a hand in Raphael's. "What is your question?"

Lash swallowed. "Is Lucifer my father?"

She closed her eyes and bit down on her lip as if wanting to keep in the answer. She took a breath and opened them, looking directly at Lash.

"Yes."

Pain flashed across Lash's face at the simple answer. "Raphael, you told me...you told me you were my father."

"I told you that I was always *a* father to you. And I always will be, no matter what," he said.

"Lucifer said he was my father. I didn't want to believe him, but something inside of me knew it was true. It's just..." he took a shaky breath and turned to Rebecca. "I don't understand. How could you...and Lucifer...you were married to Raphael! You already had Jeremy!"

Rebecca winced at his accusations.

"I'm sorry," he said, trying to calm himself. "Raphael's right. He is my father. That's all I need to know."

Rebecca got up from her seat and sat next to him, placing an arm around him. "Lahash, Jeremiel, you both have a right to know. This family's secrets have been going on for too long, and they have done great harm to all of us. Now is the time for healing. It's time you know the true story about a family of broken angels."

Naomi looked around the room. All eyes were set on Rebecca. She was finally going to hear it all. Even though she had memories of her past life back, there were still some things that didn't make sense.

She took hold of Lash's hand. With the expression on Rebecca's face, she could tell it wasn't going to be easy to hear. He looked at her, leaned in, and kissed her cheek. "Together?"

"Together," she said.

Rebecca took a deep breath and then started her story. "It all began in 1400 BC when I met and fell in love with an archangel named Raphael."

# ABOUT THE AUTHOR

L.G. Castillo wrote her first story when she was ten and has been writing ever since. She took a break from writing fiction and poetry to focus on obtaining her Ph.D. in counseling psychology. She is now a licensed psychologist and works as a professor at a Texas university. She has published her psychological research in several professional journals and books. The Broken Angel Trilogy is her first venture into publishing fiction.

### Broken Angel Trilogy
Book 1 – Lash
Book 2 – After the Fall
Book 3 – Before the Fall

### Connect with L.G. Castillo
Website: www.lgcastillo.com
Facebook: www.facebook.com/LGCastilloAuthor
Twitter: www.twitter.com/L_G_Castillo
Goodreads: www.goodreads.com/LGCastillo

Made in the USA
Columbia, SC
11 February 2025

53714523R00139